Prince of Umberlight

Book 1 in the series...
"Tales of Umberlight"

by
Alexis Fegan Black

ISBN: 978-1-942415-04-6
Eye Scry Publications

Many other Eye Scry Publications are available at a substantial volume discount to bookstores, libraries, etc. Please visit our website at www.eyescrypublications.com

For my love...
who raised me from the dead
and showed me the way back to Umberlight

Editor's Preface

This book was distilled from a collection of handwritten journals believed to date back as far as the Middle Ages. The journals were discovered among the rubble when an antiquated settlement was bulldozed to make way for a new housing development on the outskirts of London. Due to the variations in handwriting style and the exceptional length of time spanned, these writings appear on the surface to be the work of several different individuals, though analysts who have examined them have postulated that they may be the fictions of a single writer with a suspiciously long lifespan.

What is of interest is that even though the journals have been clearly damaged by time and the elements (and are therefore just as clearly not forgeries) many of the entries contain references to things that could not have been known at the time certain entries are dated. However, in light of recent breakthroughs in the field of quantum mechanics, I choose to keep an open mind, allowing myself to wonder if perhaps Umberlight is accessible to any and all who would seek her – a vast world somewhere between the scratch of the match and the resulting flame.

Liam Crocker
2015, London

_____

Prince of Umberlight

Wherein the prince must learn the art of brutality, the surrender to dark desire, and the catalytic power of love before he can become a Creator of other immortals.

**Book 2 is currently in the works
and will be released in the fall/winter of 2015.**

PART ONE
Umberlight

PROLOGUE
Now I lay me down to dream

I created this place as a sanctuary, for I am an immortal, you see, and a very long time ago the world of matter and men became intolerable to me. Certain beings – some human, others not – have asked precisely when this creation occurred, which only goes to illustrate a supremely naive misconception of the very nature of Umberlight.

There can be no *when* in a land where there is no *time*.

For that reason alone, the sun neither rises nor sets here. There are no calendars or clocks, no watches or work schedules, no hatch marks chiseled into prison walls to delineate one indistinguishable day of monotony from the next.

There is only a single moment here, existing perpetually at right angles to the dayshine world, and given the name Umberlight by one of the first Paranormals who stumbled – uninvited, I might add – into my otherwise uninhabited kingdom. It was his observation that the orange glow of the street lamps – which are powered by tiny embers broken off from the Eternal Flame – produce a warm autumnal glow that is a natural beacon, a porch light left forever on, welcoming fragile moths in gowns of colorful dust who dance like angels on the ragged hem of this night that never ends.

But back to the questions of when and how and why, which inevitably arise whenever another wayward Paranormal wanders or falls or tunnels his way into this place. If I were compelled to pin a timestamp onto the foundational cornerstone of Umberlight, it would require looking at the conundrum from the dank and dismal perspective of the mortal world – at that crossroad moment when it finally occurred to me that these human creatures whom I have been observing for centuries are, at best, only transient cattle, bumbling ignorantly toward the slaughterhouse of their own inevitable deaths. Meek sheep, lacking the force of Will which separates the herd from those who dine upon them at the end of the day.

So much comes to mind. Where to start? Do I begin by telling you that the term 'Paranormal' is intended to invoke fear for anything that does not fit into a strictly human paradigm? And yet, how can that which has existed since long before the first whining Adam and the first bleeding Eve crawled out of the primordial ooze be called paranormal or supernatural? It is merely a fact that all things come into being when circumstances are optimal and when Nature is sufficiently bored to allow some new integer into the equation of evolution. There is nothing natural or unnatural about *any* of us. Humans and Paranormals have shared this spinning ball of (b)ore since the last big bang, and the one before that, and the one before *that*.

There are no beginnings and no endings. And from that perspective, Umberlight is far more kindred with the unfathomable mysteries than anything humans like to think of as real.

But as to the question of when...

It was sometime in the late 17th century that I had finally endured more than enough of humanity. I had foolishly allowed myself to become emotionally attached to a mortal female (I hesitate to use the words "in love"), and once again I could only watch from the shadows as she became sick with age, withered, and eventually returned to the Lethe of dust. Nothing more, nothing less. The interminable and intolerable human condition.

At that time, I was not yet a Creator. I did not have the ability to transform an organic mortal into an immortal – or, at the very least, I did not *believe* I could. And that is the horror of being what I am – possessed with the gift to love more deeply than any human ever could, but simultaneously cursed to grieve more dreadfully than any immortal ever should.

And so it stands to reason it was in that same period of time that I lay myself down to sleep one particularly unpleasant morning when the sun was rising spritely and spring flowers were peeking out from wooden window boxes in every London suburb, and took my final breath of that too-bright, too-light mediocrity that humans everywhere hold in such irrationally high esteem.

I had been dissatisfied for quite some time, you must realize. It wasn't only the death of Emily that broke the remaining fragments of my heart. It was the fact that she so willingly embraced her own ending with wide-eyed faith in a mythical deity whose sole agenda was to crush the life from her failing lungs, melt the flesh from her bones with decay, and finally grind those same bones into a fine white powder with the mortar and pestle of ruthless time.

As an Englishwoman who had been infallibly indoctrinated to believe in gods and devils, Emily had wholly adopted the idea that some intangible part of herself would rise up out of a desiccated corpse, ascend into the sky in defiance of all logic, and spend eternity worshipping at the feet of the very tyrant who had given her life, caused her to suffer horrendously, and finally choked her to death on her own blood – courtesy of a disease that same entity had manifested to menace and control the population of humans whom he had shaped out of what he stated to be love.

Love?

Excuse my blasphemy, but does that make any measure of

9

sense to any rational creature?

I should warn you right now. If you are one who needs those fairy tales to get through your daze and nights, read no further, for I will openly confess I am no friend of God, no blind believer in the religious fictions Man and Church have written to soothe their fears and fill their pockets with gold coins.

I am a vampyre, if you must insist on a label. Though I will further remind you that 'vampyre' is only a word attempting to define in two finite syllables an infinite being incapable of precise definition by virtue of its very nature.

To dispel the distasteful myths...

I do not drink human blood as a necessity to my survival. I do not sleep in a coffin. I am not repulsed by garlic or crosses or silver. I have no fear of the sun aside from the fact that it is the progenitor of Time, and though I prefer the sanctuary of night, I can walk in daylight whenever I am sufficiently motivated to do so. I cannot be killed by a stake through my heart, for that heart is made of antimatter and antediluvian autumns. The body I inhabit is woven of illusion and cast into matter through my will, and therefore impervious to disease, old age, and the attempts of fearful simpletons to destroy me.

By human definitions, I am darkly beautiful – for I am also a predator, though all creatures are predators at one level or another. Since it is within my ability to be tall and lean and to wear the flesh of a strikingly handsome rogue, why would I choose to be anything other than that which humans consider irresistible, unfathomable, supernatural?

My face is a radiant flame to draw you near, my body an alluring edifice to hold you when I take you, my kiss a wicked sting that will make you want me beyond any ability to resist or reason.

I am the paradox incarnate. All that I say is truth. And every truth is a lie.

It was not always so with me. I was once human – neither beautiful nor powerful - but that is a long and sad story, not particularly interesting really. Who I am in this moment is of far greater significance, at least with regard to the tale of Umberlight and the beings who have come to inhabit her.

I could tell you that my given name was Mikal, but I was human then and it was so very long ago that even I scarcely remember that name at all. When I became an immortal at the hands of a cruel and tyrannical Creator, I took the name Thorn, for my maker had often said I was not the flower but embodied more traits of an annoying prick.

For now, I will simply add that I swear no allegiance to any deity or demon, no duty or obligation to any being mortal or immortal. This is the essence of who and what I-Am – to be whole unto myself, Knowing through Seeing that no creature is greater or lesser than any other. At the level of pure existence, we are *all* constructs of energy. This is, of course, the ultimate contradiction to one such as myself.

I-Am, when all is said and done, a being of *light*.

I have no qualms with such irony. In fact, I embrace it completely.

And that is only one reason among many that I chose to lay myself down to rest on that illumined spring morning after Emily had been remanded to the dirt. There, safe in the sanctuary of my own humble bed in an earthen basement where no light could find me, I tore my own wrist and drank deeply of my own blood – a ritual to bring visions, anesthesia to induce The Long Sleep.

And here you may cry foul, believing that I said I do not drink human blood. But remember – I am no longer human. If I drink from a mortal, it is not the rush of red that sustains me, but instead the living animus that is carried within the blood, and is as whole and satisfying in a few sparse grams as it would be if one were to drain the entire organism.

A single drop of animus (which cannot be measured in drops, of course) contains the entire living essence of the being from which it came, just as the tiniest fragment of a hologram contains the entire hologram. So to drink from a mortal isn't only sustenance for the preternatural body, it is a rekindling of the preternatural spirit, a rebirthing that is an emergence from frigid numbness into electrified bliss, and can be so overwhelming that to compare it to the convulsive force of sexual orgasm is to do it a pale injustice.

But I have strayed somewhere to the north of the point.

It wasn't only the death of another mortal lover that caused me such despair. It was fully *seeing* that the being I had known as Emily was *gone*. Into the nothing that is the marriage bed of eternity and infinity. Knowing there was no God, I knew equally there was no heaven.

And so I set for myself the task of creating one.

I set for myself the task of dreaming into being a world where death and time have no dominion.

So perhaps it could be said that Umberlight was sung into existence just *Then*, on the cusp of the Sorrowday and Hollownight.

To fully appreciate the mystery of Umberlight, it must also be understood that once something is created, it exists not only in the future, but simultaneously in the shadow of the past, as well as within the unlimited realm of all possibility – countless parallel and paradoxical Otherworlds where humans and Paranormals might find themselves if they turn left instead of right, or simply awaken in one of their own infinite other selves.

But even those words are demons of deception. What is... simply *is*.

Umberlight did not exist before that long night of my grief, but now it has always been there and always will be.

Such is the fickle nature of a laughing universe and the unshakeable Will of the vampyre who perceived himself to have been wronged by God. The fact that God did not exist was entirely irrelevant.

I needed somewhere to direct all of those feelings that otherwise dissipate and vanish into the curse of forgetting.

Love.
Rage.
Hope.
Sorrow.
Emptiness.
Winter's memories.
The poetry of fireflies.
The spidersilk of dreams.
These are the ingredients of Umberlight.

NEITHER CHAPTER NOR VERSE
The dream before the Dreaming

The altar was made of simple wood and held the artifacts and herbs required to summon an immortal. Agrimony and dream root. Chalice and blade. Scented oil.

Having lit the lantern to serve as a beacon of flame, I knelt naked and humble on the thin cushions at the altar's base, took up the small vial of oil, and applied it sparingly to my chest, careful to cover each nipple with an adequate amount to make me appealing to the dark spirits. Then to my halfway erect staff, which lengthened and grew as the oil heated in my palm.

"Vampyre, father, incubus, lover," I intoned as I had done each night for several months. "Come to me now, make me yours forever."

As I spoke the words I had gleaned from the darkness itself, my hand worked a slow and familiar magick on my body, gliding easily over my straining phallus, occasionally pausing to cup the tight twin mounds of my balls.

"Vampyre, father, incubus, lover... come to me now, make me yours forever."

I murmured the incantation for the second time, my breath coming faster as the fire in my belly burned higher.

The trick was to go slow. To focus on my intent. To tease the pleasure without indulging it too soon.

My hand slowed, though it wanted to move faster. My heart pounded, a summoning drum.

Beyond the window over the altar, the world was liquid ebony, not even a sliver of a moon on the orchards which had been in my family for generations. A flirtatious early autumn wind gripped me, running curious hands over my body until my phallus stood at full attention.

But tonight the wind which had always been feminine and sweet had turned darkly masculine and carried the sharp edge of a king's avenging sword. And whereas that same wind had remained elusive and always slipped free of my embrace, tonight that wicked elemental had taken on shape and form, and was kneeling behind me on the cushions at the window overlooking the vineyards and the distant sea beyond.

"Is this really what you want?" a man's voice whispered, so close to my ear I could taste the wine on his breath, yet so soft I could go right on imagining it was only the wind reflecting my forbidden intent back at me.

I allowed myself to imagine he was really there – something I had seldom done even at the peak of these dark rituals, for it was said that to finally believe in one's magick was to give that magick permission to believe in itself.

"Yes," I whispered. "Yes – it's what I want!"

My hand moved automatically toward my staff, but in the very next moment my wrist was seized in a powerful grip and before I knew what was happening to me, I was driven face-down onto the cushions with such a force that I thought for a moment my home had been invaded by Crusaders and I was about to be executed for acts of sorcery.

Instead, when I twisted my head around in a state of blind panic, I saw that there really was a man at my back. Not just any average human being, but a man whose face was so extraordinary it could not be a man at all. Hair darker than a blackbird's wing. Eyes so bright they had to be lit from within.

In the dim flickering of the lantern, he actually appeared to glow, his features so perfectly chiseled that I could only imagine him to be an angel – though most likely a fallen one, judging by the fact that he was completely naked and sporting a tremendous phallus that could be easily classified as a weapon.

I froze.

I could not breathe, did not dare to move.

"Do you know who I am, boy?" the man asked. Even though I was 28 at the time, I suspected that anyone under the age of at least a century or two would be a boy to this being who was, without a doubt, the answer to my dangerous prayers.

Vampyre. Father. Incubus. Lover.

"You are the night incarnate," I barely managed to murmur, more words from incantations I had written in my own blood onto the ragged papyrus of my journal. "You are the father of my death, the bringer of my life."

Words of the summoning

Words of madness.

My heart was threatening to explode, and had it done so in that moment, it may well have turned out to be a blessing, compared to what lay ahead.

"My name is Ambrose," the man said, "and I am the destroyer of your world."

Words I had imagined.

A name I had learned in my dreams.

As he spoke, he had picked up the vial of oil and poured what little remained onto the palm of his right hand, then began stroking himself with it until his evil blade glistened ominously in the lantern's pale light.

"Because you have summoned me, and because I know you are a virgin to men, I will be gentle with you this first time," he promised, though he was already prying the trembling globes of my rump apart and had placed the broad head of his saber against the tightly-clenched orifice and began to enter me.

There was no discussion, no polite dance prior to the act.

He simply did it before I could say another word.

I was paralyzed with a sensation like nothing I had experienced ever before – a devil's cocktail consisting of equal portions of fear, dread, desire and a blinding phantasm of pain that came when my "gentle" destroyer slid his well-oiled weapon so hard and fast and deep into me that I whimpered like a schoolboy and bit down on my own wrist to keep from crying out, the result being that I tasted my own blood.

Whatever sounds I made were not words – just the delirious groans and protests of a man who suddenly finds himself filled beyond his capacity to bear by the quick and merciless thrusts of another man.

It was the most horrific moment of my life.

It was the most shameful moment of my life.

And it was, without a doubt, the most strikingly <u>intimate</u> moment of my life.

Ambrose had his way with me for what must have been an hour, while I lay there on the cushions alternating between unbearable agony and intolerable pleasure I did not want to admit even though I could not deny it.

Perhaps sensing that, he held me down the entire time so that I might later have the luxury of claiming – if only to myself – that I was forced.

When his fangs cut into the tender flesh at the apex of neck and shoulder and he began drawing the living essence of me into his mouth, I experienced a single moment of true and absolute panic, for it is said that once a Creator drinks from the veins of one who has summoned him, there is no undoing the spell, no going back to the safe sanctuary of sanity and reason.

I have often wondered if I would have gone back to being just a man, but the crossroads had already been passed. The deed was done. The oath was sealed in my blood.

I belonged to Ambrose now.

He continued entering me deeply, withdrawing almost to the point of leaving me empty, then sinking in again and again until I became delirious from the ride and began lifting myself up to meet him when I sensed he was close to release.

I wanted it to be over.

I wanted it to never end.

I raised myself higher, taking the full and cruel length of him.

"That's a good boy," he murmured against my ear, reaching around my body to take my tormented shaft in his hand. "Now come with me into this night that never ends."

His skilled hand milked the liquid pleasure out of me at the same time I felt a searing burn filling me up inside, an evil fire cauterizing the lethal cut this fiend had delivered to my very soul.

"Vampyre, father, incubus, lover," I wept as his hand tightened and released around my throbbing phallus. "Come to me now, make me yours forever."

His flame burned inside me for another hour while we lay together in the aftermath, his vampyre body resting heavily on my back, his engorged manhood slowly softening inside me. When it eventually slipped free, I moaned in relief but also in secret disappointment at the separation.

"Come find me, Mikal," he commanded me. "When you do, it will be time to begin."

The wind went still.

The lantern had gone dark.

Ambrose was gone, but I knew without a doubt that I had met my maker.

~

If this story has a beginning at all, perhaps it began that night, more than eight hundred years before I met Emily, on an otherwise insignificant evening sometime in the middle of the 9th century, somewhere on my family's vineyard in Greece.

And because it was where my blood bond with my maker was first sworn, and where my commitment to obedience began, I had dreamed that same dream every night since I eventually became a vampyre at the fiend's hands.

After Emily died, I dreamt it no less than a thousand endless nights, until the moment I mercifully found my way back to consciousness and awakened into the welcoming embrace of Umberlight.

CHAPTER ONE
The spidersilk of dreams

There were tiny red spiders everywhere. They weren't just red in color, but illumined from within, glowing beings who appeared to be involved in some grand mission, each individually, and all together as a collective.

This was my first observation upon awakening from my Long Sleep. But as I sat up in my bed, it was only to discover that I was not really in my bed at all. Instead, I found myself in the highest room of a tall round tower made of all manner of stones. Pebbles of garnet, icicles of quartz. Slabs of malachite, turquoise and amber and more humble river rock, all cobbled together to create an edifice that stretched several hundred feet into the crisp night air. Yet for all its solidity of construction, it might be seen to bend gently in the wind, or twist marginally left or right for the simple joy of being a living inorganic paradox unto itself.

The bed in which I found myself was the only bit of furniture in the otherwise barren chamber, but it was of such grandeur that it deserved to be the singularity it was. Four tall posts, each the size of a giant redwood, were polished smooth as glass, and glistened in the amber glow of the full moon who had pressed her face to the window and was breathing an iridescent fog into the night.

In each of the four cardinal directions, a window overlooked the land. To the north lay the Foreboding Mountains, blanketed with the perpetual snows of mid-winter. To the south, The Forest of Turning Leaves sparkled in unending moonglow. To the west, the River of Stars promised unimaginable knowledge to any brave enough to wade in her bottomless comet-strewn waters. And to the east – the Ever-Forking Road led to the unshaped lands of All Possibility, where mazes within mazes manifested out of thin air, projected and Real-ized by nothing more than a thought; and each thought led to the next labyrinth, the next maybe, the unformed reality still in the process of its own unending creation.

At the base of the tower lay the Parish of Shadows, which could be considered the heart and soul of Umberlight if indeed a place could be said to possess such attributes. As I found myself at the east window, Smoketree Farm stretched from the base of the tower to the distant horizon. Fields of pumpkins and freckled gourds glistened in silver fog.

A scarecrow patrolled the perimeter on spindly legs of sticks that jabbered in twig-speak as he walked. Antiquated wooden windmills clattered in the performance of their duty – which was to generate the clouds and call down the fat droplets of rain which had begun to fall throughout the Parish.

These facts simply came to me, whole and undisputed.

At first, I could not fathom where I might be, but even as that thought descended, one of the tiniest of the red spiders floated down from the candle-strewn chandelier on the ceiling and came gingerly to rest on the curve of my ear.

"We have completed the basic structure, as per the blueprints of your desires, Lord Vampyre. You may, of course, fine-tune the details as you see fit," the spider said, her voice like a contradictorily deep church bell pealing in the distance. "Will there be anything else you require?"

"I am not a lord, Sister Spider," I assured her. "My name is..." For a moment, I forgot, undoubtedly a result of having slept for so very long in the span of a single moment. "My name is Thorn," I finally recalled. "And yours?"

At this, the little spider only laughed. "I have no name of my own, for I-Am *We*."

"We?" I repeated.

"We–who-are-the-architects-of-dreams," she clarified. "But no matter. I must go now, for our work here is finished and We are required at a new construction site on the eve of Yesterday."

And with that, she simply disappeared altogether, as if

she had never been there at all, and I was left to conclude that even vampyres could hallucinate in the aftermath of what amounted to a comatose slumber.

~

By mortal reckoning, it could be said that I wandered for decades through what the tiny red spider had defined as the structural blueprint of my desires. The uninhabited streets, the gold and silver rivers, the vast oceans and uncharted territories of what would later be known as Umberlight. But since time doesn't exist here, it was decades captured in a raindrop, centuries housed in a grain of sand, eternity in a speck of dust on the tip of an eyelash.

Feeling no sense of need, no hunger or desire for anything other than the visceral experience of existence itself, I walked without direction and yet with a true sense of purpose for perhaps the first time in my very long existence. Dirt paths and cobblestone streets formed beneath my feet, not leading me to follow, but following my lead. I thought of forbidden fruit, and a tree with plump ripe apples grew instantly at the side of the road, replete with a ring of magic mushrooms gathered at her base.

I was *home*. In that place which all beings seek, but few ever find – that mythical and elusive world where one simply and finally *belongs*.

I cannot tell you what I saw, for the landscape was forever changing according to an indescribable force that moved and breathed over the land without my conscious volition, yet was undoubtedly directed by some aspect of my Will which even I did not fully understand. Such is the majesty of a true dream – to bend to the desire of its creator while simultaneously maintaining the ability to surprise and amaze even the dreamer. The dream is an entity unto itself, a mirror of its own mirror, a character writing its own dialog, a contradiction without question or answer.

Deep in the Forest of Turning Leaves lay a city of skyscrapers and sprawling suburbs – yet the buildings were filled not with office equipment and cubicles, but instead housed waterfalls and jungles and the landscapes of distant planets, each on a separate floor, and each floor altogether infinite, worlds within worlds stored in a vast filing cabinet waiting to be opened and manifested. The houses in the suburbs were petite on the outside – gingerbread fairy tale cottages – yet massive on the inside, entire rooms hidden behind clear glass walls, bedroom doors opening onto ancient Egypt or Greece or the red sands of Mars.

In the foothills of the Foreboding Mountains I discovered ice dwellings and crystal palaces, sand castles in the shapes of dragons that had not been seen since long before the flood changed the face of the Earth forever. Yes, the dragons were real back then, the skies filled with them until they blotted out the sun. Or so it has been said by others of my kind who knew this world before she rolled onto her side in what is now thought to have been a polar shift.

It is impossible to describe all the wonders I witnessed upon first awakening into this place. And perhaps that is one of its finest charms – to be without limits and beyond description, to be the myth and the mystery of a dream from which no dreamer would choose to ever awaken.

I chronicled my observations at length in my journals – which had somehow found their way into my bedchamber - yet by the time I had written of the splendor of a field of peonies hiding behind a knoll in the Forest of Turning Leaves, or a single giant redwood growing along the banks of the River of Stars, the thing itself would mutate. The peonies became poppies. The redwood transformed herself to a massive Bodhi tree with heart-shaped leaves that whispered in the voice of falling rain whenever the wind blew.

Nothing was stable, yet instability was the law of any evolving universe, and so I merely observed, moving with a growing reverence through the worlds of Umberlight, making notes that were sure to read more like deranged fictions than any manner of fact.

It became my habit to sleep only as a means to enlarge the dream – to push the boundaries always one step further. Sometimes I would stand at my windows and gaze out toward the north for an eternity, imagining what might wait beyond the glaciers and snow-shrouded mountains, knowing that the thought itself pushed Umberlight larger and ever larger from the inside out, a soap bubble expanding on the breath of its maker.

Other times, I would descend the long spiral staircase and walk toward no particular horizon until the stars had spun full circle while never moving at all. The moon was always full over the forest, yet forever dark over the Foreboding Mountains. Rain was perpetually falling from illumined clouds at that point where the River of Stars emptied into the Sea of Mischief, and absolutely *anything* could be counted upon to happen or never to happen along the Ever-Forking Road. Rain here. Snow there. Once the sun even tried to break through, but was quickly slapped out of the sky by one of the longer limbs of a sycamore tree in the forest.

All of these things I perceived and experienced – not *as if* they were real, but *because* they were real.

So in awe had I become by the unfathomable immensity of Umberlight, that I once stood leaning on the blue marble sill of the window to the east and murmured out loud, "What *is* this place?"

The answer came from the wind, the rain, the snow, all of which surrounded me there at my window, whispering, whispering...

"We live in a vampyre snow globe,
where shooting stars speak in tongues
and mushrooms conspire with Grandmother Spider
to hold the dayshine world away.
Here our factories manufacture night.

Our minstrels sing lullabies
bewitching the sun to slumber.
Our heart is a cat's eye quasar,
our prince a lonesome vampyre.

This caused me a moment's pause, a raised eyebrow. "I am neither a prince nor am I lonely," I said to the sentient snowflake who had alighted on the sill and was gazing up at me with a million crystalline eyes.

The snowflake only smiled, melting. "You have visitors," was all she said just before the jealous rain swept her away.

CHAPTER TWO
The poetry of fireflies

The fireflies were the first to come – the first immortals who somehow found or created a wormhole in the metamagickal structure of Umberlight, and descended slowly but inevitably on The Forest of Turning Leaves. At first, looking out from the tower, I could not fathom what the tiny, glittering lights could possibly be. The embers which powered the streetlamps were secure. No stars had fallen. No shards of broken mirror had been scattered to reflect wayward moonbeams in this world of ever-night.

Choosing to simply *be* in the forest rather than navigating treacherous staircases and a maze of dusty paths lined with flickering streetlamps, I found myself at the edge of the trees, surrounded by the flutter of a whirlwind who brought with her a little storm of red and gold, yellow and brown and orange. The tempest engulfed me with her leaves for a moment, and then the vagabonds went skittering, their brittle boot heels clacking down the street which had turned from a dirt path to a brick road in the span of a thought.

It was after the whirlwind dissipated that I saw the thousands – actually *tens* of thousands – of fireflies. Some were resting in the trees, their combined light producing a magical amber glow that resulted in an almost pseudo-daybreak. Others flitted and buzzed throughout the forest, their tiny voices blending together until the sound was much like a haunting Gregorian chant humming in the thick autumnal fog.

To my surprise, their song had words, and the words were woven delicately into the mist, the random poetry of fireflies.

Nowhere is only a lonely city
on the lost map of Naps.
But it's all just a wizard's weaving,
in the pocket of a wicked cricket
who screams us all
into the Dreaming.

The melody was in a minor key, and only those with perfect pitch were invited to join in.

I should clarify that in the mortal world these beings are known as fireflies, but they are not really flies at all. In their natural state, they are part of the vastly diversified fairy kingdom – peculiar little immortals who have populated the planet since before the first dawn. Some like to say they *were* that first dawn, and that it was their combined light that ignited the sun and caused it to bloom. These are just rumors, of course, bold claims comprised of far more hubris than fact. And yet, the same could be said of vampyre tales, so who am I to refute the legends of the fae?

In their natural state, the fireflies are diminutive beings who, aside from their wings and minuscule stature, resemble any other humanoid species. But if captured by mortals, the firefly fairy becomes just an insect – a natural form of camouflage to guard the colony against discovery, but one that is lethal even to an immortal.

I have wept at wondering how many of these mystical beings have been captured by ornery children who put them in old jars and shake them around just to see them glow, never realizing that their thoughtless actions condemn the fairy not only to mortality, but to forgetting who and what it is, or ever was. For once changed, there is no going back, no returning to its true form.

"Actually, brother vampyre, that may not be entirely true," a voice said at my left shoulder, and in a world where I had thought myself to be the only autonomous soul. Well, until the fireflies showed up, that is.

I turned, fully expecting to find nothing but the mischievous whirlwind at my side, but discovered instead a young man who appeared surprisingly human. He looked to be perhaps 20 years of age, though it is a given that immortals – if indeed that is what he was – could take any form, and even the eldest among our kind could appear as a child if it suited them.

He wore peculiar clothing, some manner of faded and torn breeches which I would later learn were called blue jeans, and a plain black shirt with long sleeves that clung to his body like a needy lover and bore a pirate brand commonly known as the Jolly Roger. Curiously enough, I could think of no reason a pirate would choose to advertise his profession, and assumed therefore that perhaps there were other meanings of which I was unaware.

His hair was a frightful two-tone anomaly, his eyes a piercing shade of teal – neither green nor blue, but somewhere in a dangerous middle ground. Almost iridescent, those eyes were at once compelling and repelling. But most of all, it would be impossible to *not* notice that he was oddly beautiful in the same way some poisonous species of delicate flowers are beautiful.

Petite. Unassuming. *Deadly.*

Despite what I interpreted to be a challenge in both his demeanor and his off-handed comment, I did not look away. Instead, I held his unwavering gaze and gazed down at him – for he was a full six inches shorter than myself, and much slighter in build - and in that moment of feeling violated, I chose to let the tips of my fangs to show when I spoke.

"I don't suppose you would care to tell me who you are, and how you came to be in my private garden." It wasn't a polite request.

He studied me for a moment as if deciding whether to answer or bolt. He chose instead to laugh, just before he held out a delicate hand in a gesture that was all too human.

"I'm Atom," he said by way of introduction, and when I made no move to accept his outstretched palm, he came a step closer and took my hand with a grip that was alarmingly strong and every bit as cold. "And to answer your question, I followed *them*," he added, nodding his head toward the Firefly Forest – which I realized at that precise moment had just been renamed by vote of the majority of its residents. I was neither consulted, nor was my existence acknowledged at all. In a world still forming itself, such things were bound to happen.

And yet...

Another thought occurred to me, and not a pleasant one. The stars had shifted in their bed, sliding on the black satin sheets of night toward the horizon. The full moon set. Then rose again.

This intruder had brought some semblance of Time with him into my timeless world.

"Oh... *that*," Atom said with a shrug, cramming both hands into the ragged pockets of his jeans. "Time is a byproduct of light, so it wasn't me who brought it here. You could blame it on the fairies, but it really doesn't matter, as I'm pretty sure you already know."

So, this rude young whelp knew the secrets of Time. Immortals aren't affected by its ugly gravity, but instead move *between* the tick and the tock of the mortal clock. Time was no danger to us, but neither was it an ally, for its very nature was such that it eroded every organic being with whom it came into contact. Like the abrasive effect of water on stone, it battered Life until, in the end, Time would be all that remained, and the universe would be required to do yet another massive reset just to set things in motion again.

Time, therefore, was a tedious fiend, and had been intentionally left off the invitation list to my world.

"Ah, but don't you see?" the intruder said with a wide smile that revealed small white fangs not dissimilar to my own. "Even if you manage to hide here forever – whatever that word might mean – eventually it all winds back to the beginning anyway, and you have to start all over again, worlds without time, time without end, or some such bit of crappy poetry."

His bluster proved two things. 1) He could read my thoughts at least to a minimal degree; and 2) he had not a single gram of respect for territory – something every vampyre learns early on, or pays a very high price; and 3) he possessed at least a rudimentary comprehension of the tenets of metaphysics. (Yes, I realize that's three things, but as this story is about contradictions and conundrums, I shall not bother to correct myself.)

And yet, despite his air of disrespect, I found myself liking him on some fundamental level. Perhaps without ever realizing it, I had been alone for so long that any sentient company would have been a welcome diversion.

"You're a vampyre," I commented when he traced the tip of his tongue over the edge of his left fang, wanting me to notice.

He stood there gazing up at me for a blink or two, while the fireflies changed their tune and began to sing of their history, as fairies are inclined to do.

Once upon a glitch
in the wish of the Winter Witch
the first of us sprang into Be-ing
on the tip of the snowflake's prick,
while the Sea of Night was parted
and the paradox ate her tale.

Home is the leaf that never falls,
Life is the Light that never fails.
Hail! Hail!
Home is the leaf that never falls.

No one ever said fairies are scientifically accurate, and they certainly are not put off by the occasional bit of crude language.

As the song came to an end, the forest glowed with silent golden applause and the simultaneous release of what had been a breath held for too long. Legends of the fae also spoke of a world where – after countless millennium of persecution, capture and fear of humans – their kind would finally be free.

Like myself, the firefly fairies had come home.

CHAPTER THREE
How the world ends

Benevolent or not, firefly fairies can be distracting in the extreme, and so I touched Atom lightly on the elbow and inclined my head back in the direction of the tower.

"Walk with me," I suggested. In reality, I had an agenda, for underneath my calm facade, I was troubled by the arrival of so many intruders in so short a span of what should have been no time at all. I set out to know who – and precisely *what* – Atom was beyond the veil of his deceptively unthreatening appearance.

Pretending a casual detachment as he fell in at my side and we moved slowly along the red brick road in the company of clacking leaves, I asked the question that all vampyres pose to one another early on in their acquaintance.

"Tell me about your Creator, Atom," I said, fully expecting him to lie, as all vampyres do early on in their acquaintance.

Atom only laughed, though somewhat nervously. "My Creator was an arrogant ass, a monster! But I was so pathetically in love with him that I couldn't see him for what he really was." The words tumbled out in a way that seemed too much, too fast, as if well rehearsed and practiced before an audience of mirrors. "The fucker convinced me that living forever would be a hoot, and one night he came to me in a dream and turned me into... what*ever* the hell I am now."

He shrugged, laughed inappropriately again, then kicked a little green rock which was actually a raw emerald to make it go rumbling erratically down the road on a journey it had neither planned nor foreseen.

"I guess I didn't believe it *could* happen, so when I woke up like *this*... it took some getting used to just to look at my own reflection." He paused, tilted his head to the side, then added as an afterthought, "Speaking of which, I thought we didn't *have* fucking reflections!"

He did seem to favor profanity, but I thought nothing of it

anymore than I gave a second thought to his confessions of a homosexual bent where his Creator was concerned. Perhaps not surprising, as all vampyres both love and hate their makers equally – or so it seemed to *me*. In addition, gender was altogether irrelevant to our kind, and any affection came from the heart rather than whatever naughty bits dangled or nestled in one's nether-regions. I have loved men and women equally since I was turned over eight hundred years in some otherworldly past.

But the tale of my creation at Ambrose's hands is another long and sad story which I will reserve for some other time lest I wander even further from the point.

Our journey had taken us halfway back to the Parish of Shadows, and into a transition zone I had not yet spent much effort in exploring. As a direct result of that neglect, on either side of the path was only darkness – the uncharted territory of realms not yet created. Fog pressed at the edges of the lane, delicate tendrils of mist that caressed my ankles with a lover's curiosity.

Alongside the road – which had now recreated itself as a cobblestone trail that would have been very much at home in a Dickens novel not yet written – a wooden bench emerged from the fog beneath a streetlight that had not been there moments before.

Such is the magic of Umberlight – to provide what is needed when it is needed, and discard the rest to the whims of the unmanifest. The Firefly Forest lay behind us now, real to those within its realm, nothing but a thoughtform to the two who chose instead to sit on the bench beneath the glow of a single spark stolen from the singularity of the Eternal Flame.

"The myth that vampyres have no reflection is precisely that – a myth," I said, only then realizing neither of us had spoken in quite some time.

Atom grunted some manner of acknowledgement, alternating between mirth and misery. "But most myths are based in truth, aren't they?"

I smiled to myself, recalling the centuries I had spent looking for those very same answers. "The truth is that vampyres are whole unto themselves, Atom," I explained, finding him easy to converse with despite the duplicity I sensed in his chameleon-like demeanor. "That which is whole does not need to fragment itself into reflections and refractions of light in order to see itself." I paused, considering my own words, wondering if they could possibly make sense to anyone other than myself.

"I don't get it," Atom said, answering my unspoken question while swinging his legs slowly back and forth, his peculiar lace-up shoes (which were certainly not leather boots such as my own) scraping softly against the pale golden sand beneath the bench. "What does being whole have to do with casting a reflection in the mirror?"

"Absolutely nothing," I said with a small laugh – the first time in a very long time I had felt any sense of amusement whatsoever. "But what do the birds and the bees have to do with human reproduction? Myths may arise from some obscure truth, but seldom *are* truth. At best, most are struggling bits of allegory."

He didn't press the issue, just gave a boyish grin and studied me with an intense scrutiny that could have made me uncomfortable, but somehow didn't.

"I told you how *I* got here, so now it's your turn. How did *you* get here? And while we're at it, where *is* here?"

"Where do you think it is?" I asked, a question for a question to conceal my agenda.

He studied the unformed darkness, the road leading back toward the Firefly Forest or, in the opposite direction, toward the tower at the center of Smoketree Farm. He took a deep breath, though in reality vampyres didn't need to breathe at all. Like so much else, it was a habit left over from being human – and that alone told me Atom was young. Perhaps newly-turned. Perhaps only a few years a vampyre, at most.

"Umberlight," he said at last, releasing the breath slowly

as if to bring the name into being through the sound of it. "It's always night here, but never completely dark... the street lamps, you know... that glow... *Umberlight*," he repeated, almost as if in a daze.

This was the first time I actually *heard* the word at all, even though I have written it since the first paragraph of this anecdote. And so it was Atom who gave an identity to my world which had never seemed to need one before.

I didn't know whether to be amused or to feel guilty for my own negligence. Having birthed an entire world, having spun it from the raw yarn of unrelenting grief, and having woven it into being with the spidersilk of dreams, I had never taken so much as a moment to give it a name.

"You didn't answer my question," Atom said to remind me. He was a bold one.

I hadn't forgotten. I was attempting to evade an inquiry that could reveal far too much to one about whom I knew absolutely nothing.

I studied him in silence, vetting him on a level that went far deeper than the five physical senses could reveal. I was looking *into* him – not reading his mind but examining his *intent*. It wasn't so much the question of *how* Atom had come to Umberlight that disturbed me, but *why*.

At first, he seemed oblivious to my probe, but then he looked at me with those disturbing teal eyes, ducked his head as if expecting me to believe he was shy, and gave an incongruous giggle. Yes, a giggle.

"You know, if you *really* want to know what makes me tick, why don't you take me back to the tower and have your darkest of dark ways with me, Thorn?"

He didn't wait for my answer, and indeed I'm not sure I would have had one, for his lewd suggestion did have the uncanny effect of taking me off guard. Not because I was offended, but because I came from a place and time where long courtships and hesitant kisses generally preceded the more coarse machinations of the mating dance.

Then again, as I have already revealed in the brief tale of the dream of meeting my maker, vampyres are often impatient creatures who simply ask for what they want or take it without even bothering to ask at all.

I settled on a more immediately pertinent question. "How do you know my name?"

Clearly choosing to ignore my inquiry, Atom hurried on. "Oh, don't look all sour. It's not like you haven't thought of it – bedding me, I mean – and I'm sure you're not a virgin. Hell, there are legends about you to this day! Which brings me to the real reason I followed those infernal fairies into this little paradise of yours."

I could only stare at him, trying to decide which of his ludicrous comments to address first. It occurred to me that I could banish him altogether – a thought alone could send him spiraling into the land of the sentient dead which resided at the bottom of the River of Stars – but for no logical reason, I actually liked the little bastard.

That thought was perhaps more disturbing than anything he had said, for I did not *want* to like him. Feelings of affection on any level were far too dangerous, as I had most recently discovered with Emily, and though Atom *appeared* to be a young and mischievous vampyre, I knew better than most how deceiving appearances could be.

Since it seemed he was offering to answer my unspoken question, I began there. "And why *did* you follow the fairies, Atom?"

His responding laugh was entirely genuine. "To find *you*, of course," he said, and had the audacity to punch my arm in what was meant to be a gesture of good-natured playfulness.

I am not particularly good-natured.

And again, his response generated far more questions than it answered. Not wanting to give him the satisfaction of knowing he had hooked my attention, I looked away and maintained an air of indifference.

"And now that you have found me, what is it you want?" I

paused for a moment, letting him think he was getting away with something, and then I pinned him with a menacing gaze that had stopped more than one mortal heart. "And how *do* you know my name, Atom?"

He gazed out over the unmanifest darkness for some time even though Time was bending and swaying and not at all stable. Eventually, it went back to sleep, leaving the stars still in the sky, the moon in fog-shrouded penumbra.

"There's not a vampyre on Earth who doesn't know your name," he mumbled under his breath. "But so far this place is just a myth even among the myths themselves. Everybody *believes* in Umberlight, but nobody has ever seen it." He seemed to pat himself on the back, then added with an indulgent grin, "Well, until me, that is. I opened the door to vampyreland for everybody!"

His words carried darker implications which caused me to immediately say, "You can't bring mortals here. *Ever.*" Even I wasn't entirely certain where that leap to conclusion had come from, but once the words left my mouth, there was no reconsidering them.

"Oh? Why ever not?" He didn't seem disappointed as much as genuinely curious.

"Mortals are the repositories of death. They bring the disease with them wherever they go."

"I see," Atom mused, rubbing at the sparse blonde stubble on his narrow chin. "That could be a problem – because as you've probably figured out by now, there are a lot of Supernaturals who have been hunting this place and want to come here – a *lot*. And when they *do,* the humans won't be far behind. Can't be helped."

The moment Atom and the firefly fairies arrived, I had abandoned any hope of keeping Umberlight as a sanctuary solely for myself. On some level, perhaps I was even relieved at the prospect of companions. So I simply said, with bold conviction intended to stave off his protests, "I have no problem with other immortals, Atom. But humans can *not*

36

come here. Their presence alone would forever alter the fundamental nature of this place."

Atom sighed and kicked at the little green and gold pebbles lining the path. "Then you'd better start building fences, my friend," he suggested with a giggle that sounded all too deviously elfin. "For aren't humans the most curious creatures of all?"

He had a point, but I had prepared for that well in advance. "The fences are already in place. They are the walls of perception, the barriers and shields of belief."

Atom looked perplexed. "In English? Or at least High Fae?"

It had been too long since I spoke High Fae, so I opted for English. "Humans seek only what they already know to be true. This place is built of the fibers of myth and the woven mist of dreams." At his perplexed stare, I simplified it considerably. "Umberlight does not exist to them because they do not *believe* it exists."

Atom remained unconvinced – it was evident in his demeanor – but he let it go and fell into a lengthy silence as I contemplated what he had said.

"Supernaturals?" I repeated at last, breaking the stillness which was breaking itself as rain began slowly falling, fat silver drops plopping into the crannies and crevices in the cobblestone road.

"Paranormals," Atom clarified. "The label changes every century or two."

Like a small human child, he held out his hand into the storm, tilted his head backward and extended his tongue to catch a passing raindrop. Savoring it with closed eyes, he gave a smile that was undeniably serene, even content.

"It seems so..." *real.*

Though he never finished his sentence, I heard his unspoken thought.

I allowed him that dalliance, a rare luxury to find even a single moment of such abject perfection – though such moments were less rare in Umberlight than in the World Above.

"You said you came here to find *me*," I reminded when he opened his eyes – though now he was drenched through to the skin while I remained altogether dry.

Atom grinned, observing the difference between us. "How do you *do* that?"

I had never thought of trying to explain it, but was motivated by the challenge. "I-Am the rain and I-Am myself. That which *is* the rain cannot be affected *by* the rain." It occurred to me then, "It's the same with Time. That which *is* Time cannot be weathered by Time." It wasn't much of an explanation, but it seemed to satisfy him.

When he did finally speak, his voice went soft, barely a whisper. "I want you to turn me," was all he said.

At that confession – which I perceived to be absolutely authentic – my head jerked toward him as if on a string, and I could only stare at him with the disdain one normally reserves for animal droppings on the bottom of one's shoe. It was not even my choice to have such a reaction. It simply came of its own accord, for if there was one thing I knew, it was simply this:

"I am *not* a Creator." I said this with emphasis, though not unkindly. "And even if I were, you are already a vampyre. One cannot be turned who has already *been* turned." It was a given. Why he would even suggest it was a mystery of profound proportions.

Atom gave his characteristic shrug of one shoulder, and kicked at the ground again. "Yeah... well... when you asked about my Creator, you should have asked his name."

One of the most annoying things to a vampyre is the feeling that someone is intentionally manipulating him while simultaneously wasting his timelessness.

"I don't understand."

Again he breathed deeply. Again he chose some innocent pebble on the ground and kicked it until it skittered across the lane and disappeared into the nothing on the other side. Where it landed, a dead tree sprang to life. I don't mean it was a dead tree that came *back* to life. It just grew there in an instant – spawned from the seeds of anger and irony, a misbegotten still-born child of chaotic energy.

The rain fell harder.

Not wanting Atom to realize the extent of his own power – which appeared to be quite formidable – I said again, "What are you trying to tell me? *Who* was your Creator?"

"The fucker's name was Atom," he said at last, then waved his own words aside with an impatient gesture before hurrying on. "I'm trying to tell you that I turned *myself*. In a dream, I mean. I came to myself in a dream and did the whole ritual and when I woke up, I was *this* me instead of *that* one."

Finally I understood. Atom was mad. Certifiable. The primary ingredient of grandma's holiday fruitcake.

Despite that conclusion, some tiny grain of truth glimmered through whatever he was trying to say.

"You mean this literally, don't you?"

If what he said were true, the implications were potentially world-shattering. If a human could will his own energetic Other to make him immortal, it would change the structure of the human race – *and* the vampyre race – forever.

When Atom didn't answer except to look at me with a raw expression that revealed the fear behind his bold facade, I felt something within myself begin to shift – and it was not a shift I would have chosen, for it was one that could soften me far more than I would ever care to be.

He was vulnerable. And he was scared.

And he needed me just as I had once needed Ambrose.

"You're saying you summoned your energy body into your dreaming and it knew the ritual for transmogrification?" I had heard of such a thing only once, but had presumed it to be another allegorical myth of self-actualization – another in a long list of self-aggrandizing lies proclaimed by my own Creator.

39

He looked at me with a desperation normally reserved for condemned prisoners on the morning of their appointment with the gallows, then abruptly grabbed me by the arm, hanging on for what I do believe he perceived to be his very life.

"I *need* you to turn me, Thorn!" he persisted. "I mean – I need a *real* immortal to turn me for *real*!"

I almost felt sorry for him – for certainly he believed what he was saying. His grip on my arm was so intense he would have drawn blood if I were mortal.

I placed my hand over his, met his eyes, and did not look away.

"You are *already* a vampyre," I repeated calmly. "Even if what you are saying is true, what has already been done cannot be done again."

He shook his head the way a small child might. "You don't know that – not for sure," he insisted. "I'm a vampyre for *now*, but am I really *immortal*? And the *real* question is if it can be *undone*!"

Atom was proving to be a master at contradiction while the mist at the edge of the lane crept closer to listen, now obscuring the path almost entirely.

"Did you not just say that you wanted to be turned?" I asked. "And now you are saying you want it to be undone? Or that you *don't* want it to be undone?" I didn't bother pointing out what I had already concluded. He was insane. It was the only safe conclusion – though I must admit I did not like myself much for *needing* such a conclusion, particularly when the very possibility was unparalleled.

That thoroughly intrigued me, and in doing so it also hooked me.

Releasing my arm, he took a trembling breath, then leaned back on the wooden bench. Time passed. Or didn't pass. With the increasing fluctuations, it was hard to tell.

"Look," he said at last, struggling for some manner of calm as he spoke with his small hands clutching the front edge of

40

the bench. "What I'm trying to say is that I *like* being this way and I don't want to go back to being just another dying, rotting mortal."

"It doesn't work that way," I assured him. "There is no going back."

And yet, how many times had *I* longed to return to my mortal life, only to eventually acknowledge that it couldn't be done? Finally, having accepted what I-Am, I came to cherish the passing of the centuries, the turning of the pages of the mortal world. Despite the pain of it, despite the curse of loving and losing far too many, I had finally fallen in love with the thing itself.

I was *immortal*.

I liked being who and what I-Am. How could I blame Atom for feeling the same?

Opening his eyes at last, he pinned me with that disconcerting gaze. "Why do humans die?" he asked unexpectedly.

It was a question I'd posed to myself countless times. "Because they *believe* they will – because it is ingrained into their belief systems before they ever draw their first breath. It is the primary tenet of The First Fundamental Lie[1] – and it is precisely why humans can never be allowed in this place."

"Okay," Atom concurred, seeming momentarily surprised by my response. "So here's the rub, Thorn. I was *human* when I

---

[1] **Editor's Note:** Elsewhere in the unpublished segments of these journals, a reference was discovered which was apparently the author's attempt to explain "The First Fundamental Lie" to an apprentice. It read: *The human paradigm is built on the false notion of Time, and so it could be observed by one outside of the matrix that the entire paradigm is erroneous because it has created within its subjects a viewpoint that is based on what immortals call The First Fundamental Lie. Think on this, for it is only when you are willing to sacrifice The Lie that you will be able to glimpse these fundamental elements of creation which are channeled through your essential be-ing pure and limitless, but limited entirely by The Lie which was designed to do just that. Ironic, yes? You are made of the pixels and photons of limitlessness and timelessness, yet unable to access that nature because the nature of any consensus is to create parameters which can only limit the power and understanding of the thing itself.*

dreamed myself a vampyre – and *because* of that, somewhere in my programming I have human *doubts*. Do you see what I'm getting at?"

I did, and at the same time, I did not see at all. "Continue," I suggested cautiously, intrigued with him despite my better judgment.

He gave a heavy sigh, tapping one foot on the ground as if trying to drum up an answer. Finally he got up and began to pace in an altogether human fashion, his odd shoes squeaking as he scuffed them along the damp cobblestones in the winding road.

"This isn't some decision I made lightly, Thorn," he said, almost to himself. "I hounded it for years – everything from Carlos Castaneda to quantum mechanics to religion – and what it all comes down to is that we *are* what we *think*."

While I had no idea who Carlos Castaneda or Quantum Mechanics may have been, I was familiar with the quote from Buddha. Perhaps the *only* thing I learned from my own Creator was embodied in those words.

We are what we think.

It was then that something became clear to me as I really looked at Atom through a completely neutral eye. His manner of dress. The odd style of his hair, which was spiked at the top, blonde at the tips and black at the roots.

"Where are you *from*, Atom?" I asked, not in an attempt to derail his impassioned fervor, but because I really did want – *need* – to know.

His eyebrows furrowed. His head tilted in the manner of a perplexed puppy. He said, "Los Angeles?" as if asking my permission.

The fact that I had never heard of it should not be surprising. When I left the world of matter and men and entered into the Long Sleep, the year was 1670. Los Angeles did not yet exist.

Atom and I looked at one another. And for the first time, *he* seemed to notice that my appearance was considerably different from his own.

I had awakened in Umberlight looking exactly as I had on the day Emily was laid to rest, on the day when I had stood in the sheltering shadows of a willow tree while a storm dropped rain on the small gathering of mourners gathered next to an open grave.

On that day, I had worn dark leggings which would have been more appropriate in the previous century, a thin white poet's shirt and a black leather coat. My boots were of a sort considered outdated at the time, but I had not been a wealthy man during those years, and so I may have appeared ragged around the edges, even if undeniably handsome.

I had taken to wearing my hair tied back with a plain ribbon and tucked inside the billowing confines of my shirt, for it would have fallen to mid-back if left to its own devices, and in glossy black waves that would have posed a serious threat to my anonymity. Long before I became an immortal, I was often told that my eyes were hypnotic, and though one might expect a vampyre's eyes to be dark, mine were a deep shade of olive green.

When I looked at Atom and saw how fundamentally opposite we were, I could not deny that we must be from two different worlds altogether.

It was the shoes that gave it all away. Those funny contraptions that squeaked when he walked, laced up like a lady's corset, and appeared to be sewn together with patches of mismatched color brighter than any burst of spring flowers. What was even more odd was that they came all the way up to his knees, and were adorned with some peculiar metal gadget up the back.

He caught me looking at his feet, and gave a laugh that may have been self-conscious. "They're called tennis shoes," he said. "I only bought 'em because they zip up the back. And besides, the guys at the club thought they were hot."

My look of confusion caused him to add, "They get me laid."

Judging by the crude gesture which accompanied his statement – inserting his right index finger into a circle of thumb and forefinger on the left hand – I surmised he was referring to sexual gratifications. And, if I was not mistaken, sexual gratifications with other men.

He became more intriguing to me after that, though I refused to admit it even to myself.

In addition to his strange manner of dress, I could see no practical reason for his hair to be two radically different colors, and fashioned in such a way that it stood up from the roots and looked as if he had been struck by lightning. Clearly, Atom was as alien to me as I would have been to an aardvark.

"What *year* is it where you are from?" I asked, realizing as I posed the question that it could put me at a distinct disadvantage. Nonetheless, it was unavoidable.

Atom and I stared at one another for what might have been centuries had time held any meaning. Finally, seeming to come to a decision to trust me, he said, "2015?"

How does one process that kind of information? On the one hand, I could surmise that my Long Sleep had been considerably longer than I had imagined. On the other hand, I already knew there was little correlation between time on Earth and the timelessness of Umberlight. Daylight there was evernight here. The idea of tomorrow did not exist here, but had always been some fanciful goal to most ordinary humans over 'there'.

If I didn't worry the math too closely, Atom was from a space/time roughly 345 years in what would have been my future, if I had had one.

And while I wanted to ask him about his world and all the mysteries and miracles that must certainly be contained within it, I was far more interested in one simple thing.

"If what you say is true, then how did you come to be *here*?"

Atom had stopped his pacing and came to sit once again

at my side on the bench. "Would it mean anything to you if I said I was doing research on the nature of wormholes in the quantum structure of space-time?"

"No."

"Well, to keep it simple, I've always believed – I mean since I was a little kid – that there are other worlds all around us," he explained, his voice taking on an intense passion. "And for every world that exists, there are millions – actually an infinite number of millions times a million – of parallel or alternate worlds."

Humans of my day believed much the same, even if expressed in different terms. Rumors of the fairy realms. Legends of undersea kingdoms. Myths of vampyres. In Umberlight, that uncertainty was expressed along the Ever-Forking Road – where every manifested reality led to every *unmanifest* possibility.

"Go on," I said.

We spoke of wormholes and quantum apples and infinite improbabilities for what must have been weeks on that night. With no sunrise or moonset to dictate where rational conversation began and common sense ended, we were free to indulge every thought, and eventually we both came to acknowledge that the questions far outweighed the answers.

Atom explained that he had been a malcontent and even a misanthrope in his world. *That* was no surprise, but I came to realize that he had also been a *seer* – one who saw the world far too clearly, but held no particular power to *do* anything about it.

What I learned from him about the world of 2015 was both fascinating and terribly frightening – for one thing was certain: even as much as the humans of my day were largely asleep on their feet and going through the motions dictated by their religions and their culture, the humans of Atom's time were even more akin to what he referred to repeatedly as 'zombies'. They weren't just asleep on their feet. They were the walking dead – a reference Atom seemed to find deeply amusing, though he never said exactly why. And far worse, they were destroying their own environment in a way that would lead to their own extinction sooner rather than later.

When I reminded him that it was not his responsibility to change the world, I found him in complete agreement. And that's when he began to expand on exactly how – and *why* – he had gone down the rabbit hole of what he called 'a quantum application of shamanic knowledge.'

What this boiled down to was a thorough and unshakeable comprehension of something vampyres have always known and mortals have always suspected. The thing which humans call their soul is more accurately what mystics might call the dreaming body – a quantifiable vessel of energy that can be projected out of the physical shell and into infinite otherworlds. For most humans of *any* period in history, that projection is limited to dreaming or to the occasional out-of-body experience.

In the human world, these experiences are explained away, disregarded as unfortunate lapses in reason. The unrelenting voice of the dayshine world has made certain of that, for the one thing any consensual agreement can ill afford is a population that embraces its own power – so it's no surprise that what should be *common* knowledge has become *forbidden* knowledge, and not even I can remember a time when that wasn't so.

What mystics know is that this dreaming body is the potential vessel of one's immortality. The trick – and it *is* a trick - is to transfer one's awareness from the mortal meat suit into the immortal Other.

Other than Atom and the unreliable and unlikely claims of my own maker – it is not a feat that can be accomplished by wishful thinking alone, no matter how sincere or focused the wisher may be. It requires a Creator – one who is both an accomplished *seer* as well as an insane magician. One who has the ability to move the *essence* of one's humanness out of its organic container and conjoin it to the indestructible Other.

46

And yet, what I learned from Atom – if I believed him – was that he had spent decades nurturing his infinite Other, courting it, wooing it with everything from poetry to rituals. And though I never let on, the rituals Atom had devised to seduce his Other were virtually identical to the chaos magick I had used to summon Ambrose.

He had even built an altar where he would leave 3 drops of his own blood in a glass of red wine every evening for a period of time spanning twenty years. For the first 19.5 years, absolutely nothing happened. Then, one morning, he awoke to discover the glass empty.

He made it abundantly clear that he had *intentionally* projected his Other as a vampyre with the power to transform his mortal self into an immortal. He spoke at length, and in impassioned words, about how he had lured his dreaming body into the physical world, and how he had even become lovers with it after it began to drink the wine he left for it on his altar.

He addicted it to *himself*.

I had never heard of such a thing, but the universe is vast and I'm certain there are many things I have not yet encountered. Whenever I had tried to press Ambrose about his wild claims, he had always avoided my inquiries until, one day, he warned me that I must never speak of it again.

Atom made a convincing argument. He told a tale of how he had seduced his twin in the same way a mortal would seduce another mortal. In that way, he hadn't been lying when he had said he was in love with his Creator to the point of being blind to all rationality.

According to Atom, the courtship between them went on for several months – during which time the Other (whom Atom had taken to calling 'Zen') would come to him in the night, and in between their acts of intimacy (he spared me no detail), they would always share what he called 'a kiss of the blood.' Atom would cut Zen's wrist with a ritualistic blade, drinking deeply of the silver animus of his immortal vessel, his darker intent being to pull the Other into himself completely.

The problem came when Atom began to insist to Zen that it was time to complete the transition. Of course, what every vampyre knows is that one's maker tells *him* when it is time. While the mortal may believe he or she is ready (as if one can *ever* be ready for such a thing), the truth of the matter is that most die in the fall between their mortal death and their first immortal breath.

Despite all of Atom's shamanic knowledge and quantum awareness, neither he nor Zen possessed the secret of precisely *how* it is done. And though I had no reason to doubt him when he spoke about the epic love affair between them, love alone was not enough to bridge the gap between what it is to be human and what it is to become vampyre. Had Zen been more fully developed, or had Atom been more patient, perhaps things would have turned out differently.

And yet...

The end result was that Atom did manage to draw the immortal essence of Zen into the mortal shell of himself – which, of course, is precisely the *opposite* of what must happen.

What resulted was that his aging process slowed considerably and even reversed itself to a point – for I also learned that he had been a man of 43 at the time his transition occurred. But even though he now appeared as a young scoundrel of no more than 20, what*ever* manner of body he inhabited *was* slowly aging.

What was troublesome to me were the intrusive thoughts suggesting that *somehow* I should be able to correct his potentially fatal error, yet for the eternal life of me, I could think of no way to do it, nor – coldly – any reason why I *should*.

As I have already stated, I am not a Creator. Fewer than one vampyre in a thousand possesses that ability, and though I had desperately longed for it when Emily was taken ill, it did not come at my bidding, did not answer even the most mournful wail of my grief when I knew I would lose her.

I came slowly out of my contemplative state when Atom fell silent. The rain had paused, and through a gap in the clouds the stars shone like sequins sewn into the fabric of the night.

We had begun walking again, and were coming into the outlands of Smoketree Farm. The tower was peeking out above intermittent layers of silver cloud and amber fog. In the distance, the scarecrow sentinel continued his endless vigil over damp pumpkins and empty streets.

"Okay, I have to ask," Atom said as if suddenly needing to change the subject. "Why pumpkins? Did you grow up on a farm or something? And what's with that creepy scarecrow? Hell, that thing scares even *me*!"

He was an inquisitive little intruder, yet I didn't mind his questions.

"Pumpkins are sentient observers, receptacles of Knowledge," I said, though whether my statement was true or only a pleasant fantasy, even I was not sure. "At any rate, I did grow up on a farm of sorts – a large vineyard in Greece." I paused, looking out over the somber drizzle and the vast expanse that was Umberlight. "As for the scarecrow, I did not consciously will him to be here, though I find his presence comforting."

Atom seemed perplexed, staring at the ground as we walked. "But if you didn't call him into being, who did?"

It was a good question. "The spiders, I presume."

Fortunately, Atom didn't pursue it. We had come to the base of the tower, which was swaying ever so slightly in the cool aftermath of the storm, and leaning more than may have been wise in any other world toward the north.

As I had always been alone in Umberlight, there were no ominous doors barring the entrance to the tower, no iron bars, only a stone arch that opened into a massive foyer where the spiral staircase ascended past treacherous landings and rooms that had hidden themselves and balconies that appeared and disappeared of their own accord.

Normally, I would have just willed myself to be in my austere room at the top of the tower, but Atom did not possess the ability to transport himself with thought alone. So we climbed the stone stairs in silence until we came to a landing three floors from the top.

There I stopped, seeing that a new room had formed in the time I had been away. The workings of magic. The transmutation of thought or need into the material realm.

"You may rest here for as long as you need, Atom," I told him. "But eventually you will have to return to your own world."

My tone left no room for disagreement, though it did surprise even myself. A moment before, I had been contemplating ways to save him. In the next second, I could only think of needing him to be gone – for despite whatever brief moments of empathy I may have experienced, I was by nature a solitary beast who had no desires or delusions to right the wrongs of all the worlds.

I did not always like that aspect of myself, for it was a trait handed down to me by my own maker. *Some things can't be fixed*, Ambrose had warned when I had lamented to him about a dying beggar who came to the gates of the estate for food and was turned coldly away. *And what you can't fix, you have to cut loose so it doesn't drag you down with it.*

And while I had taken to slipping the beggar bread from the pantry where food for the mortal slaves was stored, Ambrose had considered me a weak fool for my sympathy. In fact, it may be one reason he was harder on me than with the other dozen or so fledgling vampyres housed on his large estate.

As for Atom's response to my declaration that he must leave, I had expected an argument or at least some grimace of protest. Instead, he only shrugged one shoulder and gave a smile that was meant to be seductive.

"So, will you turn me?" he asked as if requesting nothing more than a penny's worth of sweets.

"No." I'd already explained to him why it couldn't be done. And even if it *could*, my answer would have been the same.

He didn't press the issue – though I knew that time would come. "Can I sleep with you – just for tonight? Just sleep. I promise."

"No." He was young and he was clever – which meant his promises were written on water with disappearing ink.

It is undoubtedly clear to you that I didn't entirely trust him. But at that moment, I must also confess that I did not entirely trust myself. It wasn't that I wanted to bed him, as he had so ineloquently put it. But the presence of another soul after so long alone was a temptation I did not care to indulge.

In hindsight, I have often wondered what harm it might have done, but at that moment when my mind was still reeling from the arrival of the fireflies and the unexpected intrusion of this seductive halfling, I said goodnight to him without any further conversation, and then retired to my own bed chamber.

Perhaps not unexpectedly, a thick wooden door with hasp lock had formed in the short time it took for me to walk to the east window, survey the glittering stillness of the fog-shrouded fields, then turn toward the bed.

I summoned thirteen candles – three on each rain-damp windowsill and one in the center of the room. And then with a trembling hand, I locked the door.

The world as I had come to know it was ending.

CHAPTER FOUR
Serpent in the garden
Deal with a devil

My Creator was an eccentric man even among other vampyres, so it stood to reason that Ambrose had collected exotic trophies and souvenirs of the places he had traveled. One of those souvenirs was a Persian leopard he had acquired in exchange for granting immortality to a Turkish prince. At the time I was turned approximately one year later, the cat had barely reached adulthood, and took a liking to me during the years I was forced to live at my maker's immense estate on the shores of the Mediterranean Sea near Piraeus.

The cat did not perceive vampyres as either threat or food, and so it was not uncommon for me to awaken during my rest to find the large feline draped across my legs or pressed against my back, at times behaving in such a manner that I came to believe he perceived me as another of his own kind.

There is no real point to that small anecdote except to say that when I awoke in my bed with the candles having burned low and the rain now pattering insistently on the tower's weathered green copper roof, I did not think it odd to feel Hades curled against my back in proper cat fashion.

But as the haze of sleep dissipated and I came to full awareness, I bolted up in the bed to discover that it was not my old friend who had climbed in to share the night, but instead the young interloper whom I had come to know as Atom.

I thought – *hoped* – that I had dreamt the entire chain of events. The arrival of the firefly fairies. The erratic movement of time in my timeless world. Rainbow corset tennis shoes. Atom. All of it.

But as I scrambled to my feet and stood looking down at the naked waif sleeping on his side in my bed, I could only try to squelch the automatic cry of dismay that rose in my throat. Despite my best efforts, however, a small gasp broke the silence and caused the imp to stir.

Impulsively, I threw a blanket over him – though I had never owned a blanket since becoming a vampyre. I simply had no need for one. Until now. The fact that it was soft and made of fur only made it all the more disturbing.

Atom sat up and rubbed at his eyes the way a child might. Then, seeing me standing next to the bed, he clutched the blanket tighter to his chest and actually seemed to blush even though it should have been biologically impossible.

"What the *fuck*?" he squawked, shooting me an accusatory look. "Damn, Thorn, you could have asked, and you already *know* I would have said yes! I like a little kink as much as the next guy, but – *damn!*"

Ah. So now it was *my* fault that *he* had climbed into *my* bed.

And yet, when I looked at him, I realized he was innocent. It was evident in the fact that his aura did not fluctuate even when he was flaunting that very innocence.

"How did you get in here?" I asked anyway.

He seemed about to accuse me of some heinous sorceric trickery, then thought better of it. "I don't know," he said. "Last I knew, I was in bed in my room."

I looked around to determine if anything else was out of place. The heavy oak door was still locked. There were no fairy footprints on the windowsills. The scarecrow was at the farthest edge of the Parish, tending to the hemp seedlings and picking magic mushrooms.

Looking at me, Atom frowned. "Do you always sleep in your clothes?" he asked out of the blue.

In the world of Umberlight, they weren't clothes at all. They were thought-forms. Manifested memories of how I had looked on the day Emily was buried. And those memories were superimposed onto the energetic structure that was my preternatural body. None of it was real, yet all of it was far *more* real than anything in the real world.

"Do you always *not*?" I countered.

He had no response, just glanced rapidly around the room as if searching for his misplaced garments, which were nowhere to be found.

What caught my attention when he turned his back to me for a moment was the jagged scar which ran diagonally from a point just below the left shoulder blade all the way to where the right kidney would be in a normal human body.

But vampyres had neither kidneys nor scars, and that alone caused me to wholly acknowledge that Atom *was* still in some sort of quasi-physical form. If *I* chose to move among humans, I would appear as solid as any of them, but I could turn to smoke or vanish altogether with nothing more than the thought of doing so. My form, therefore, was the perfected manifestation of how I saw myself – at least that's how Ambrose had once explained it to me on the rare occasion when he had explained anything at all.

You are what you think, and who you eat, he had said with a sardonic laugh.

But younger vampyres who had not yet settled into their preternatural forms *could* find themselves vulnerable to stakes or beheading or sunlight or a large knife inserted into one's back. As Atom had intimated: doubt could kill and beliefs were potentially lethal. The immortal who *believed* himself mortal was walking a dangerous tightrope between two divergent worlds.

Perhaps he did have some reason for concern when he had lamented about the possibility of returning to his mortal human state, and the fact that he had crossed my path made him – *somehow* – my responsibility. There were no rules or laws saying so. It was merely a philosophy I had come to live by after over eight hundred years of trying to deny it.

He was evolved – perhaps far beyond anything I had ever encountered – yet at the same time, he was not *changed*. He had transformed, but had not transmogrified. He had dragged his immortality into himself instead of surrendering himself to his immortality.

I rubbed at a spot in the center of my forehead – a habit I'd had as a human when I was prone to headaches. Perhaps not surprisingly, a chair with thick burgundy cushions had appeared next to the bed, and I sank down onto it as my mind raced in every known direction and found new ones that hadn't even been mapped.

Atom was going to be a problem. *My* problem.

A *big* problem that may not be possible to solve.

Why did I care?

Because he had made me like him.

It was that simple.

~

"What if I told you you could have her back? Or any of your old lovers, for that matter?" Atom asked.

I was not easily fooled. "I am not easily fooled. What is dead is forever dead." And yet, I myself was living proof of exactly the opposite.

Atom only shrugged. "Maybe," he agreed, "or maybe not. You're still thinking with your linear mind. But time is more like a sphere or a bubble than a line. A hologram."

I had no idea what he was talking about and said as much with a look.

We had been sitting underneath the sheltering Bodhi tree on the west bank of the River of Stars, our feet dangling in the cool waters while we gazed into the fathomless depths where galaxies swarmed like nests of hornets and rogue comets took aim with the precision of a big blue shooter marble at distant worlds where children were eating breakfast and mothers watched the sky with an ever-fearful look, waiting, always waiting for their world to end, too.

I should point out that I had nothing to do with what went on in the River of Stars or along the Ever-Forking Road. These were the realms of the unmanifest, where gods and destinies (if either existed at all) played with themselves *ad infinitum,* just to see if they would go blind.

Even if I had wanted to change the course of an asteroid or cause a world to be born here or there instead of somewhere else, that was not within my power. And though I had never enjoyed being out of control, there was a certain comfort in knowing that not everything which resulted in chaos, mayhem and destruction was my fault.

"It's like this," Atom insisted, determined to explain his crazy idea even though I had expressed a preference to sit in silence and watch eternity unfold. "Because we're outside the hologram, what it really comes down to is that we have *access* to the hologram at any point. The past and the future are all happening at once – or you could even say they've *already* happened, and the hologram of time is just a storage cell for every moment that ever was or will be."

I felt that headache coming on again. But despite myself, I couldn't help feeling intrigued. Atom was a brilliant theorist, and there was a certain dark poetry to his suggestions which I'm not sure even he realized.

If what he was suggesting were true, a man could attain considerable power and wealth in the mortal realm just by having foreknowledge of certain events. Knowing the outcome of a horse race could generate a fortune. Knowing how the cards were going to fall in a game of high-stakes poker would bring even more. The ability to manipulate financial speculations could give a man the wealth of Midas, the power of Zeus.

The possibilities were endless.

And while I had never sought after such goals in the World Above, it was largely because I had never had them, nor even desired them. It wasn't a moral issue. I had simply never had a reason to care.

And yet...

The idea of being able to step back inside this hologram Atom spoke of, at some moment in time when Emily was still young and vibrant held more appeal than I dared to examine.

"Tell me again how it would work," I said, distracted as a wayward speck of stardust floated to the surface of the river and nibbled at my toes.

"Think about it," Atom said with a wicked grin. "You can go fuck around with humans to your heart's content if that's what you want, and if you ever *do* have the misfortune to fall in love again, you'll know *how* to turn them so you don't have to watch the meat suit fall off their rotting bones."

Somewhere in that logic was a gap comparable in size only to the abyss between galaxies.

"I hardly see how returning to the World Above would gift me with the knowledge – let alone the *ability* – to transform a mortal into an immortal anymore than going to a museum would turn me into a master painter," I pointed out.

Atom gave a heavy sigh. "For a guy who breathed a whole fucking world into being, you can be a real stick in the ass, Thorn."

I had been called worse.

"Sometimes you just need to trust the process – it's the only way you ever really learn anything. Isn't that what *you* said?" he persisted.

I had no recollection of saying any such thing. "You have me confused with Figment – a little voice who lives inside your head and sings lyrics of lies while calling them truth." It was a slightly more polite way of saying – again – that Atom would have been very much at home in a home for the mentally deranged and may indeed have escaped from one.

At this, he picked up a fist-sized rock from the shore and threw it into the River of Stars, disrupting my reverie when waves of ripples distorted the view.

I realized he was staring at me with a fair amount of ire, and for that reason alone, I pretended not to notice.

I should point out that this type of exchange between us had been going on for quite some measure of whatever Time had come to mean in Umberlight – whether months or decades, I could not have said. But one thing was certain: it always ended the same way – either Atom stalked off, somber and sullen, back to his room in the tower... or I did.

"Why don't you stop being such a dick and just admit you're scared, Thorn?" he said. He'd said it before, sometimes with slight variations on the analogous synonym. Sometimes I was a dick. Sometimes a prick. Whatever word he chose, it was always a crude reference to a man's penis. The willie. The tool. The root of all evil. I had given up trying to keep track of his vulgar vocabulary.

Being a patient man, I waited until the ripples on the surface of the river had stilled. Not much had changed during that time. A galaxy or two had collided, one eating another with typical cosmic irony. Two planetoids in the space between Earth and Mars had collided, resulting in a vast ring of debris. Stars had fallen while others were being born.

"I created this place so I *wouldn't* have to deal with the World Above, Atom," I reminded him. "And were it not for your presence, this would be a peaceful – and *private* – sanctuary."

I said this without raising my voice, with no animosity whatsoever. Atom, on the other hand, was still young enough and human enough to react with anger, which is perhaps what I had been manipulating him to do, for it was often the easiest way to get him to reveal whatever secrets he had been hiding since his arrival in Umberlight.

"You're a real fucker, Thorn!" he said, though he hadn't *yet* begun to shout. "You may have created this place as a sanctuary against death, but when you moved in and slammed the door behind you, you stopped *living*!"

He was getting better at trying to get under my skin. "I'm not inclined toward a dualistic fatalism. It *is* a choice, you know."

He quirked his upper lip in an expression that said he had no idea what I was talking about.

"One does not need death to validate life," I explained in short syllables. "Life *can* exist without death."

"You're lonely, Thorn," he countered. "And you're bored."

"Assuming either were true – which they are not – what does that have to do with *you*? Why would it be any concern of yours at all?"

"I care about you," he said, all soft and fuzzy.

I laughed out loud. "You want me to turn you," I corrected. "When I tell you I do not possess the ability, you ask the same questions again and again, hoping the answer will be different even when you know it will always be the same. *That* is the very definition of madness."

He was silent for awhile. A merciful reprieve.

Finally he said, "Are you so afraid of failing that you won't even *try*? Are you so cold that you'd just let me die? And you already know I will if *you* don't do something!" But he didn't wait for my response. "All you can think about is how you're going to get back to the World Above and get your dick in your chick, and you're *better* than that, Thorn! You may *think* you love her, but *I* think you're thinking with the wrong fucking *head!*"

To my surprise, I felt a rush of real anger threatening to rise up in me – a sensation I had seldom experienced since the night I finally fled from my own cruel Creator.

Holding myself in check, I spoke very softly. "You would be wise to mind your tongue."

But he only laughed. "Yeah? Is that so?" He poked me on the arm with one bony finger, clearly attempting to incite me. "Well here's the rub, fucker, so listen up! You can go back and bump smuglies with some skinny English bitch if that's what you really want to do – but you can't *get* there without *me*, because that's what *I* know that you *don't!*"

At this point, I did have to laugh. "I can return to the World Above whenever I want." I had never tested it, but it was intuitive and intrinsic knowledge.

"I'm sure you can," Atom agreed. But he poked me again with that annoying finger, which I did consider biting off, I admit. He leaned closer and put on his best attempt at being menacing. "But you'll just bounce right back to where you started from – right back to the sad, sad day when your girlfriend had the bad manners to grow old and croak. Right back to your shitty little basement in your shitty little flat when you finally had the gumption to *do* something other than just wallow in the fucking misery of the fucking mortal world!"

He barely paused for a breath, then rattled on. "What you don't seem to *get* - oh great and wise wiseass! – is that you're still locked into your linear idea of time. And worse, you're still tied up in the dungeon of your own self-imposed limitations – and until that changes, you'll always go back to your last *linear* memory and Emily will always be dead by the time you get there! You don't know how to wake up in the *yesterday* instead of always stuck in the tomorrows!"

He stopped for just long enough to poke me on the arm again, his eyes glittering with rage as they bored into mine. "You keep saying you're *not* a Creator, and for as long as you believe that, it'll go right on being your impotent reality!"

What happened next was largely a blur.

It wasn't *what* Atom said or even the manner in which he said it. Instead, it was the unmistakable *truth* in his ramblings that brought me to my feet. His words weren't just words. They were imbued with images and packets of additional knowledge and information neither spoken nor even intimated, but all of which pointed to one thing:

I was being blackmailed.

For he was right about one very important matter: I could navigate Umberlight and move in and out of the World Above, but I did not possess the secret of how to navigate *time* as it related to the mortal realm.

If I wanted my Emily back, Atom held vital information I would desperately need – or so he liked to claim. Whatever else Atom may have been, he was a living-dead-anomaly – and anomalies had a tendency to throw very large monkey wrenches into extremely delicate machinery.

Before I understood what was happening, I had dragged the young miscreant to his feet and slammed him up against the base of the Bodhi tree.

"What is it you *want* from me, Atom?" I demanded, barely an inch from his face, which looked at close range, very delicate and practically elfin. "I've told you that I can't change you and yet you keep insisting I *must*! You. *Are*. Insane!"

I might have launched into a lengthy soliloquy about rationality and accepting one's limitations – for there are some things that cannot be changed, cannot be fixed – but even as I heard myself preparing to speak the words, I realized they were the very things I had fought against for longer than I cared to remember. They were the cornerstones of the human agreement and, as such, they could become coffins even for an immortal. Another lesson I had learned from Ambrose.

Madness, it seemed, was dangerously contagious, and Atom was the blue ribbon winner in the category of Crazy.

The fact that he was right never entered my mind just then.

Our eyes had locked in an unrelenting battle, our minds clashing against one another like two gladiators poisoned by testosterone and some innate need to win, even though *what* one might win could never be properly defined.

It wasn't that I didn't *want* to help the little bastard with his self-induced problem. I truly did not know how, and that realization awakened a fury in me the likes of which I hadn't felt since Emily died. Even as an accomplished metaphysician who had breathed the worlds of Umberlight into being, I was still altogether powerless against the one thing in all the worlds that had the audacity to haunt me still.

Death – the hag-bride of Time.

He was my nemesis, and as Atom had often said, I was his bitch.

That is what outraged me. And *that* is what made me grab him by his scrawny shoulders and shake him until I was certain I heard his bones rattle.

"I can't *save* you!" I shouted at him. "I can't do what can't be–"

"I just want you to *try*," he said, interrupting my rant in a voice that was barely a whisper, and as painfully raw as any utterance I had ever heard. "At least *try*, Thorn. *Please*. I don't know how much time I have left, and I don't want to die."

And before I knew what was happening, he had leaned into my formidable wrath and kissed me with the affectionate openness of a lover. Not a quick brush of lips against my cheek. Instead, it was the kind of kiss one anticipates after a long courtship – not probing or deep, but a slow and delicate exploration of lips that have wasted too much time talking and are finally ready to acquiesce to a language beyond all words.

I was so shocked by this development that I allowed it to continue longer than I might have preferred had I been thinking clearly. I wanted to tell myself it was only because I had been alone so long, but that excuse was becoming tired and worn even to my own ears.

He wasn't aggressive. Nor was he shy. He simply encouraged *me* to take the lead or to push him away. And though it might have been more prudent to shove him into the river and drown him there, I found myself leaning into him as my fierce grip on his shoulders relaxed into a less bone-splitting pressure.

Every thought I had ever had throughout my very long existence went skittering through my mind. I was being seduced by the serpent in the garden, who was simultaneously blackmailing me to perform a task that was altogether impossible.

And yet...

In that moment when all the worlds were still and silent, in that moment when autumn was shedding her colorful gown like a virgin on her wedding night, I could only think that I did not want to go on being alone – certainly not forever – and certainly not in *that* particular moment.

As I leaned into Atom and our bodies pressed full length against one another, I could feel the strength of his arousal as it strained against the ragged blue jeans he always wore. And though I am made of star dust and the quantum filaments of my own Will, I felt myself responding as if I were human again. I hardened as a man would. I breathed in sharply as a need I did not know I possessed overshadowed my reason.

With my human lovers, the physical aspects of passion were always eagerly anticipated, even frenzied at times, but they were not like... *this*.

This was somehow... *primal*. For despite the fact that Atom was seemingly flesh and blood, he was also *vampyre*. And I had not coupled with another vampyre since I was forced to submit to Ambrose so long in the past.

Forcing thoughts of my Creator from my mind, I allowed myself to fall deeper under the spell being cast by the night and the crescent moon reflected in the river, and the little imp who had opened his lips to me and was encouraging me to penetrate his mouth with the tip of my tongue.

While we lingered there beneath the sheltering branches of the tree, our kisses deepened and heated. He moaned when my hand slid down his chest, moving lower to cradle in my palm the straining shaft of him, and had I not held him pressed to the base of the tree with my own body, I do believe he would have collapsed when I first touched him there.

I did not have it within me to be gentle with him, for even though he had aroused my passion in a way I had not felt in longer than I could remember, he was also operating with an agenda. And so even as I was wanting him, I was also wanting to hurt him in some entirely human fashion which might serve to remind him that *he* was the intruder in *my* world.

Without any pretense at tenderness, I tore open his jeans and slid them down his narrow hips until his phallus was exposed to me – bobbing and straining at its own prison of pink flesh until it must have been exquisitely painful. Another cry came from his lips, and I kissed him hard and deep to silence him – and though he tossed his head from side to side to evade my advances, there was no denying it was exactly what he wanted me to do.

And if it *wasn't* what he wanted, it was too late for negotiations.

With one hand, I grabbed his hair and held him still, sliding my tongue over the sharp point of his small fang until I felt the preternatural skin tear, and we both tasted the immortal essence of my blood. I knew the effect it would have on him for the same reason I could not help recalling the effect Ambrose's blood had had on me the first time he had kissed me in such a manner.

Atom's head arched back. His entire torso trembled, convulsed. I took his ample shaft in the palm of my other hand, milking it until it bled the pale white essence of Life.

He drew at the cut on my tongue, drinking me deep, and then he screamed with a release that left him practically fainting.

But I was not done with him.

I allowed him to suckle at my blood for a moment longer, and then I took him roughly by the shoulder. "You will turn around and present yourself to me," I said, my lips pressed close to his ear.

He drew a sharp breath, eyes going wide. Was it a look of fear, or one of relief?

"N-no!" he stammered, and he was so very *good* at the game that I couldn't be certain if he wanted me to spare him or if he were pleading with me to torment him *more* before finally having him.

I had given him my blood, my animus, the very *force* of my life. If he really did want me to try to turn him, as he had said, this was how it must be. It was all I knew. It was how Ambrose had turned me.

And so I injected my tongue into his mouth once again, feeding him a taste of eternity, feeling his manhood soften in my hand, then instantly harden again. Tears ran down his face – not tears of blood, not the silver tears of animus, but the clear and perfect tears of human cataclysm spawned from a passion too fierce to contain.

With a thought alone, I found myself naked there on the west bank of the river, our reflections captured in the water's resplendent mirror.

Atom was looking, too, and seemed to pale when he realized precisely what was about to happen, when he understood the price he was about to pay for daring to make a deal with a devil.

"Turn around," I demanded again. Not waiting for him to comply, I took him by the shoulders and spun him about until his small round rump was suddenly pressed against my impatient blade.

Leaning against the tree for support, he wept openly when my hands parted the trembling globes, though he made no attempt to evade the savage thrust that lifted him onto his toes and would have caused a mere human to pass out. I withdrew just as quickly – eliciting a mournful cry from deep in his throat – and then I entered him again with equal ferocity.

As the second thrust sank even deeper than the first, I bit down hard on his pale neck, my fangs automatically finding the artery that carried the heart and soul of him through veins that were alarmingly human and just as undeniably vampyre.

The taste of him was carnal apple red, an erotic symphony of dark melodies, the twisted poetry of one who was hopefully and helplessly in love with the pain that only being taken forcefully by another man could deliver.

And so I gave him what he wanted – withdrawing completely, thrusting deep and hard without warning, withdrawing again before the feeling of fullness could bring him to satisfaction. All the while, I was suckling the raw nectar of him to satisfy a thirst I had no longer known I possessed. As I drank my fill from him, I teased him with the thick tip of my phallus, threatening a promise he already knew I was sworn to keep.

Now he was whimpering in little gasps that sounded like a wounded animal, but I knew the wound was not fatal when he arched his back and tried to impale himself upon me.

To punish the demon, I slapped him hard across the right buttock – a blow that sounded like a tree branch snapping and elicited a wail of surprise that caused him to lunge forward in a failed attempt to avoid a second blow that landed on his left cheek.

He had raised one arm to serve as a cushion between his head and the tree, and as I spanked him twice more on each trembling cheek, he wept piteously into that arm with the sheer pleasure of the pain itself.

I took him again – plunging mercilessly into him until he was impaled so deeply that he began to speak in tongues. With his free hand, he tried to touch himself to hasten his release, but I would not allow it. Seizing him by the wrist, I forced his arm behind his back as I once again deprived him of my blade, and slapped him hard across his already-tormented buttocks.

"You will endure this for *my* pleasure," I told him, biting again at the lobe of his ear.

When he had stopped sobbing after the last cruel blow I dealt to him, he nodded sharply into his arm, snuffled once, and barely whispered, "It hurts." Another softer little cry, then, even more quietly. "It *hurts!*"

What he *really* meant – there could be no denying it by the way his hips were undulating and his breathing was coming faster and faster – was that it hurt to be *empty*. It hurt in *between* the blows I had dealt *far* more than the blows themselves. It hurt to *not* be ravaged, both inside and out.

To soothe that anguish, I ran one hand over the quivering mounds with a tenderness that was more torture than not. He writhed and begged me to kill him.

Instead, I entered him again without gentleness – hard

and fast and with an increasing cruelty that lifted him off the ground. His knees had gone weak, and when even the Bodhi tree could no longer hold him on his feet, I picked him up and lowered him onto the thickest and most cruel hilt of my weapon, and there I held him for a very long time.

When I returned him to his feet and allowed him a moment to breathe, he once again made the grave error of attempting to pleasure himself, and once again earned the wrath of my hand against his quivering buttocks. The burning sting of it was so intense that it caused him to cry out with a howl that chased away the stars and echoed all the way to the Foreboding Mountains.

It went on like that until he had climaxed twice more – the last series of spasms so forceful that they captured me inside him and milked me until I filled him with another injection of my immortal extract, just as Ambrose had filled me more times than I could recall, in acts just as brutal, just as merciless.

After I had climaxed deep inside him, I allowed our bodies to become separate once more, then immediately turned him around to face me, cupping his head in one hand and bringing his lips to rest against the firm mound of my flat male breast.

"Drink," I commanded him. "Quickly!"

He was eager. And he was hungry for me.

The tips of his fangs were sharp and without forgiveness as they cut into me and he began to draw hard on the living animus. In order for a Creator's essence to work its magic, it had to be ingested while the mortal's blood was still alive inside the vampyre body – giving the human his own blood back, filtered through immortal veins and forever altered – and since I had drunk so deeply of the imp, I could feel the restless spirit of him coursing through me like a thousand hummingbirds thrumming their wings in every inorganic cell of my body.

The thing about vampyre blood is that it is a powerful

aphrodisiac but also a potent anesthetic.

Within moments, the demon was hard again, but at the very same time he had fallen deep asleep in my arms.

I knew I did not possess the power to turn him – at least not yet, and probably I never would. But all he had asked of me was that I *try* – and in exchange for the information he claimed to possess, I would have fucked my father's only son in front of an audience of nuns.

So much for my pompous integrity – worth not a single gram of gold when compared to the agenda that motivated me more than anything ever had.

I lay him down to sleep in a comfortable nest of fallen leaves, and then I plunged headlong into the icy waters of the River of Stars, where I floated in the sheltering arms of a nebulae for a very long time.

I learned a great deal about myself that night, not the least of which was that Atom brought out the beast in me. What I did not yet fully understand was *why*. Yet it was clear to me he had intended the events that had just occurred to go through the motions of actually occurring.

All I knew about turning a mortal into an immortal came from what little Ambrose had revealed so many centuries in the past, and even then it had been couched in veiled terms and analogies I could scarcely remember.

I could not begin to fathom what in all the scattered worlds had just happened.

I only knew that I *liked* it.

I liked the *power* I held over him.

I liked the *pain* I forced him to endure.

I liked the pleasure I *permitted* him to have.

I liked the very idea, however remote, that I *could* be a Creator.

~

If I had been human, I would have said that the next

68

segment of timeless eternity was spent in fever dreams. Possibilities unfolding. Agendas forming. Secrets whispering about themselves but never coming clear.

He is not what he seems.

But who ever is?

I was in and out of awareness, having drifted unwittingly into the one realm that is potentially lethal to any conscious being. I have come to call it the land of the sentient dead – a non-place, non-time Neverwhen where one is aware but totally without identity, without any sense of cohesion. And yet, there is no "one" at all – no *self* in the land of the sentient dead, and so there is no presence of will even to raise oneself *from* the death of whatever awareness existed prior to that dissipation of self-awareness. The paradox is not only self-replicating, it is also paradoxically self-*destructive* in that realm, and so it exists merely as another nothing in a grand cotillion of Absolute Nothingness.

In the land of the sentient dead, existence becomes nothing more than a series of meaningless observations, no matter how profound or life-altering the event may have otherwise been. The birth of a star has as little significance as the death of a loved one, for there is no unique point of view to admire the birth or mourn the death.

As Thorn, I had heard of this dastardly state of being in myth and legend. As the minuscule bit of awareness floating *within* it, there was only the distant knowledge that I did not want to be "one with the All" as so many hocus pocus religions liked to encourage.

There was something within me that was *me*. A spark of life. A demand for a perspective that was unique unto itself – not merely an observer of the All, but an active participant and even a key player in the grand scheme of things.

Unlike the tiny red spiders who were happy to be *We*, there was the uncompromising will to be *me*.

More than simple arrogance, it was my *right* – the right of all beings, but the manifestation only of those who *choose* to invoke it with all the infinite power contained in a single particle of light.

The only way to describe it is to say that raising oneself from the land of the sentient dead requires an act of pure will the likes of which some ancient scribe was attempting to describe when he wrote of God shaking off the cloak of darkness and proclaiming with a shout of spontaneous parthenogenesis–

"I Am!"

I said the words aloud, though at first they were a muted and irrelevant whisper. The All all but laughed at me.

Every nonexistent nanosecond was an eternity as the "I" struggled up from the depths, and was simultaneously pulled back down, only to struggle up again in a battle that seemed to go on forever.

"I-Am!" I said again, and this time it came in a voice I vaguely recognized as my own.

And then someone was shaking me, small hands on my shoulders, warm breath on my neck, close to my ear.

"Wake up!" a man's voice commanded in a tone that left no room for argument. "Wake the fuck up, goddammit, Thorn!"

At the sound of my name and the persistent hands shaking me without any pretense at gentleness, I sucked in a harsh gasp of air the way a newborn takes its first breath, and then I cried out in a shout that was undoubtedly heard all the way back to the mortal world...

"I-Am!"

~

Why did I tell you these things? How are they relevant to the story?

For one reason and one alone.

Only after the events which had not yet begun to unfold, and which I will begin to reveal, was I able to look back and realize it was probably the very moment when I became a Creator.

And yet... there are many moments and many ingredients that go into creating the power of creation.

My journey toward wholeness was only beginning, and I was so deeply buried in it that I could not *see* it at all.

CHAPTER FIVE
The Art of Brutality

When my disorientation dissipated and I was able to sit up, I realized we were back in the tower, and I was in my own bed, fully clothed and covered with a warm fur blanket, even though my last previous memory had me stark naked floating in the River of Stars.

At first, I believed it had all been a dream, a terrible dream... or was it a wonderful dream? But when I saw Atom sitting on the edge of the bed, the memories came flooding back with an intensity that left me momentarily speechless, and very well may have caused me to blush had I been capable of such a typically human response.

I had always been a gentle and considerate lover. And yet, if reality were any reflection of my recollections, I had savaged this little imp so fiercely that he had passed out in my arms, and I myself had fallen into a coma from which even most vampyres never awaken.

I opened my mouth to offer some halting apology, but it died before it was ever born when I remembered exactly how *much* I had liked it. Not only had I enjoyed it physically, but on a level I could not even begin to understand, it was as if something had awakened inside me – some previously unacknowledged beast who would not agree to be put to sleep like an ailing pet.

And so it was that newly born beast who sat up in my bed, breathing in the crisp, cold air that smelled of ripe pumpkins and sweet musk and early apples.

I didn't need to ask the obvious question. Atom hadn't carried me back to the tower in some noble act of chivalry. It was simply how things worked here – often in ways even I did not yet understand. Just as I had awakened in my bed once before to find him pressed against my back, so it was that now we were back in the tower because that is where we needed to be.

The metamagickal forces of Umberlight clearly wanted us together – though for what purpose, no one could have said at that point.

I sat in silence, remembering for no particular reason my last day on Earth as a mortal. Though snow in Greece was uncommon, I had awakened on that morning to find the world covered in the white icing of virgin silence. I had never met Ambrose in the flesh, though I had dreamed of him countless nights. I was 28 at the time, and had lost my beloved wife and only son to some passing sickness three years before.

It was then that I began summoning the immortals, saying my prayers of vengeance to the creatures of the night itself instead of making offerings to the old gods who had gone deaf long before I was born. It was then that I made the unwavering commitment to live forever or die trying – and so it stood to reason it was then that I began courting the shadows and imploring them to grant me immortality so that I might spend all of eternity tracking down and slaughtering whatever demon or deity had seen fit to introduce Death into an otherwise magnificent paradise.

Ironically, it had snowed on that final morning of my human life – for it was on the evening of that day when I met Ambrose on a dark street, and was taken to his large estate where I would be granted my wish, even though I would end up pleading with him to spare me or to kill me before the events required to fully turn me were completed.

As I sat there entertaining a memory I did not choose to remember at all, it began to snow in Umberlight – dusting the fertile fields of Smoketree Farm in a pale gown that glowed silver-blue in the moonlight. The wooden windmills had gone still, their broad paddles frosted in ice. The scarecrow had tucked himself into an otherwise empty barn for a long winter's nap.

The beauty of it was so idyllic that I might have sat there on the bed forever absorbed in its allure, but I became distracted by Atom's squirming as he struggled with the broken zipper on his jeans. I remembered then that I had torn his trousers open with little regard for their frailty, yanking them down to his knees for no other reason than to satisfy my own indulgences.

Upon waking, I had been embarrassed at my actions, at the cruelty of my own need which had surfaced like a starving monster from the depths. But now, the beast who had awakened within me only smiled, looking over my shoulder like a ghost in some gothic novel.

I ignored him for a moment, focused on the man-boy sitting at my side.

You should comfort him with kind words to atone for your actions, my common sense advised. Irritant though Atom could be, he didn't deserve what I had done to him.

The beast had other ideas. *You must teach him discipline and submission,* it countered. *The first lesson you must learn if you want to be a Creator is the art of Brutality.*

My common sense was righteously outraged. *Brutality is a purely human trait,* I protested with indignation. *Inexcusable!*

The beast only laughed. *Think about your words. Is it not true that one's maker must be brutal enough to take a life before he can have the strength to summon that life back from the dead?*

What occurred out there in the wilderness had nothing to do with taking his life, I argued with my Self. *What I took – quite by force – was my own selfish pleasure.*

And is it not true that sex is only a living allegory for Death? the beast countered reasonably. *If you do not have sufficient brutality to take what you want from him – teaching him to submit to you so that he does not resist at that crucial moment when he is suspended between life and death – how do you think you will ever have sufficient brutality to actually kill him, just as your own maker killed you?*

Creation must be an act of love, I argued, suddenly *wishing* I could change the past, *wishing* Ambrose could have loved me as I had once believed I loved him.

Love is only one integer in the equation. The beast said this with absolute certainty and a complete lack of interest in my angst.

And what are the others? I asked when it became clear he had no intention of discussing my tragic past.

Brutality is the first, the fiend within me said as if discussing nothing of greater significance than a grain of sand. *Dark desire is the underlying force – the second gate through which you must pass. And then there is love. Without all three, you will never hold the power of a Creator.*

I liked Atom a great deal. But I was not in love with him. Far from it. In fact, after what had happened, I found myself close to loathing him for his role in seducing me.

Who seduced whom? the beast inquired, though it wasn't a question. *You may pretend not to see your own beauty, the power of your allure, but if you are not aware of the effect you have on others, you are dumber than we both thought.*

I wanted to say, 'Fuck you,' but that would have been a knee-jerk response worthy of Atom as well as a suggestion to simply crawl off in a corner and masturbate.

Instead, I mumbled under my breath, "Go away."

Ah, but you know what happens when I do, my other Self reminded. *Without me to ground you, you end up in the land of the sentient dead. And who knows? Next time you might not be able to scream yourself back into being. Next time I might just leave you there forever.*

Whether I liked it or not, he had a point. And for the record, I did *not* like it in the least.

A part of me had awakened that I had been suppressing for centuries. Calling him 'the beast' wasn't far from the truth. But his real name was Power – an aspect of myself I chose largely to ignore because of the power Ambrose had once held over me.

This entire dialog and its accompanying revelations took place in less than a moment, while Atom sat there fiddling with his zipper and casting glances at me that were either accusatory or beckoning. With Atom, one could never be certain. And still, I held a growing empathy for him, and for his predicament. In his quest for immortality, he had trapped his eternity within the finite confines of his own mortality.

The irony was beyond ironic.

The reason he is <u>in</u> his current predicament is because of his arrogant over-confidence, the beast advised with no hint of mercy. *Now is the time to explain it to him.*

Explain *what*, I did not exactly know – but the beast took control before my common sense could regain the upper hand.

At the foot of the bed, a simple robe of black silk had appeared by the same force of magic that had returned us to the tower.

Standing, I picked it up and handed it to him while he looked up at me with a perplexed expression.

"This is what you will wear while you are under my stars," I informed him in a voice that *sounded* like my own, but in words that took me entirely off guard. "Whenever I ask it of you, you will – without argument or hesitation – kneel and present yourself to me for the taking."

Atom seemed genuinely surprised, maybe even fearful. Then he only grunted with a sarcastic inflection. "Why not just keep me chained to the bed, naked?"

I leaned close and took the lobe of his ear between my fangs, threatening to draw blood but reneging on the promise at the precise apex of pain and pleasure. "I find it more to my liking when I ask you to lift the robe and you are forced to submit."

At that, he actually paled.

And so I began explaining "it" to him in a torrent of sudden knowledge I had not possessed before, but which was now every bit as much a part of me as the certainty of my own name. I simply knew these things without knowing *how* I knew them, and could only surmise they had been somehow injected into me while I slept in the unbeating heart of the land of the sentient dead.

"If you are sincere in your desire to be truly immortal and to undo the damage you have done to yourself, the ritual of transformation must be performed three times within the span of a single moon cycle," I began, daring for one horrific instant to remember my own dark submission to Ambrose, longing to forget, knowing I never would. "But since there are no such cycles in Umberlight, you will submit yourself to me whenever I ask it, no matter what the circumstances.

"In addition," I said before he could protest, "you must understand one thing, and understand it very clearly – for you have already taken a dangerous step toward your own obliteration."

He looked up at me with those illumined teal eyes. "I don't understand," he murmured. "What step? And while we're at it, I thought you said you *can't* turn me. Why the sudden change of heart?"

"You compelled me to try," I reminded him. "And now that we have taken the first step, I am bound by my own agenda to determine if it may be possible."

This seemed to give him some small measure of relief. "Oh," was all he said. Then, after a long silence, "Good. That's good."

I laughed out loud at his false bravado. "It may not be as good as you think," I warned him, once again recognizing that the beast within me knew far more than was available to my immediate awareness. "For as brutal as our first joining may have seemed to you, the next two times will be worse. *Far* worse, Atom. And here is where I would caution you to be mindful of your words, no matter how terrible things may become."

His elfishly handsome features had turned somber. "What are you saying?"

When he tried to turn his head to look out the window, I took his chin in my hand and forced him to look at me when I spoke. "Do you remember what you said to me during our joining?"

To my surprise, he still had the capacity to smile. "I said a lot of things – not all of them were in English, as you might remember." A pause, then a soft-spoken whisper, "I *wanted* it. Exactly like it happened. I *wanted* it to be like that between us, Thorn."

I grudgingly had to admire his raw honesty. For even though I had fought Ambrose and hated Ambrose and wanted to kill Ambrose for the sexual cruelties he had unleashed on me during the rituals of my transformation, there was a part of *me* that had wanted it, too. There was a part of me that wanted someone else to take control, a part of me that wanted to be taken with an unrelenting force that might shake me out of the polite niceties of the traditional missionary position and the lazy slumber that always followed in the aftermath of having methodically serviced even a wife whom I had truly loved.

But the beast did not speak of these things, for to do so would have made me more vulnerable to Atom than I wanted to be.

"You asked me to kill you," I reminded him.

When I released his chin, he ducked his head and gazed at the stone floor for a long time. "I remember," he said at last.

"You must never utter those words again," I cautioned him. "For if you do – if you ask me three times to end your life, I will be obligated to do so."

The same warning Ambrose had given me. The same warning I had foolishly ignored.

Atom looked up at me with an expression that hovered somewhere between terror and relief. "Why?"

"The ritual of transformation holds the power to make you immortal," I said, though it was really the newly-awakened beast who spoke through my lips. "If you cannot withstand the torment of creation, you will certainly not be able to endure the torment of immortality itself."

Atom seemed predisposed to argue. "Yeah, but, just because I *ask* you doesn't mean you have to *do* it."

"Ah, but it does," I said, knowing it to be true, both on an intuitive level as well as from direct personal experience. I had begged Ambrose to kill me the first time he forced me to kneel and give myself to him. I had pleaded with him again to end my life when he came to me and initiated the second ritual. And had I not been gagged and bound, I am certain I would have asked again for him to kill me when I was forced to endure the torments of the third and final ritual.

"Why?" Atom said again. "I mean – it's not like anybody is standing over you with a gun to your head. So *what* if somebody asks you to--."

I placed my index finger over his jabbering lips to silence him.

"It is simply known that a Creator who would allow a weak and unfit spirit to become immortal would no longer *be* a Creator, but just another impotent vampyre, forever grieving those he has loved and lost with no power to change it." I paused, then added, "This is the way of it. This is the law of our nature."

Sacred words. *This is the way of it. This is the law of our nature.* I did not know where those words came from, but I knew their truth, felt it all the way through to my dark and eternal soul.

Something had changed within me.

Instead of sharing my awe at this knowledge, Atom had the audacity to extend the tip of his tongue to press against the finger that was resting across his mouth. The sensation was both erotic and threatening to my control. I wanted to pull away, but chose instead to allow him his insolence. It would be one more reason to punish him later.

"So it's all about *you*," he surmised, intentionally taunting me.

My smile showed him my fangs, a reminder of what I would do to him. "Of course."

"So let me get this straight," he said, and took my finger in his mouth, suckling on it for a moment as our gazes locked. I trembled internally at the intimacy, though I never let him see what his advances were doing to me. Eventually, he lifted his head and added, "If I ask you three times to kill me, are you saying you actually *will*?"

"I am."

"And you really *would*?"

"I would have no choice."

"And I've already made the big boo-boo once?" he said, as if to clarify it for himself.

"Yes."

"So if I said to you right now – 'Kill me, Thorn' – that would be twice?"

The little bastard did like to test his boundaries.

"Words spoken without intent are only noise," I reminded him. "It is what you say – or don't say – during the rituals of transformation that will determine your fate."

He considered that in silence for a moment. "And what makes you think I was serious when I said it while you were fucking me?"

His coarse choice of words was meant to shock me. I didn't allow it. "You meant it," I said, with no doubt. Through the synergy of our joining, I had felt the pain I caused him. Enough pain for him to *want* to die, just as I had wanted to die when I had surrendered the virginity of my back side to Ambrose.

He challenged me with his eyes. "But how do you *know* I meant it? Can you read my mind?"

I had to acknowledge that I couldn't. But I didn't admit it to him. When I had taken his blood, I *should* have been able to know him as intimately as I knew myself. And yet... that was not the case.

Brutality, the beast said, drawing me from my quandary. *Don't let him corner you. Take the lead. Take control!*

I was not obligated to answer Atom's questions – for once he had made a pact with me to become his Creator, he had abdicated all personal rights until such time as the ritual was complete or the contract was mutually dismissed or the candidate was true-dead as a result of the ritual itself.

"Take off your clothes," I commanded him.

He was not quick to comply.

"Why?" he asked with that teasing grin. "Can't get enough of me?"

While Thorn might have been amused, the beast was not.

"Take off your clothes," I repeated, more forcefully. "Do not think for a moment to question my commands."

This seemed to amuse him. Or maybe it actually aroused him. He stood at the edge of the bed, hesitated for a moment as if testing me, then slowly removed the black shirt with the Jolly Roger symbol, and let it drop to the floor. Then, sitting, he unfastened his absurd knee-high tennis shoes and tucked them under the bed.

When he stood to remove his pants, all he had to do was let them fall, for the fastening was entirely destroyed, and so they pooled at his ankles in a puddle of blue, leaving him naked as he stepped out of them and stood there looking at me with an expression that was both defiant and uncharacteristically shy.

The flickering candles in the chandelier threw a warm golden glow over his body, recreating him as some sort of cherubic angel or lost duke of an ancient fairy tribe. The fact that he was erect only added to his splendor, but it was not my intent to have him again so soon.

I nodded toward the black silk robe which he had left lying on the bed when I told him to undress. "Put it on," I said.

Our eyes locked and argued. Wars were fought in that gaze.

Finally, he looked away and turned to pick up the robe. Without any further discussion – verbal or otherwise – he shrugged into it and tied the sash at the waist. Then he was back to staring at me with that insolence which lay at the very root of *why* he was in the mess he was in. In that way, my beast was correct. Atom was going to have to learn to fine art of submission.

And the robe was where he would start. The design was such that the lowest part of his cheeks were always visible – to me, to the massive mirror that had appeared on one wall of my bed chamber, to the scarecrow sentinel, the firefly fairies and any other creature, organic or inorganic, who might pass through the worlds of Umberlight. In addition, the front of the robe overlapped only slightly, and would part as he walked to reveal the state of his manhood – whether erect or flaccid. At that particular moment, as already mentioned, the little imp was noticeably aroused, and anything but 'little'.

This, I had learned from my own humiliations at the hands of Ambrose, was altogether normal during the cycle of one's creation. Despite the cruelties one's maker might unleash upon him, one was nevertheless in an almost constant state of arousal. A few vampyre philosophers liked to claim it resulted from the prospect of awakening in an immortal body, while most vampyres simply accepted it for what it was.

The rituals of transformation were both unforgivably cruel and indescribably *erotic*. One craved the maker's brutality while at the same time weeping piteously at the torture of it – a perfect pain equally physical, mental and spiritual. A torment born of futile resistance and nurtured through the acts of being forced – literally *forced* – to accept into oneself the living animus of eternal *Life*.

It was the pain of coming undone, the beauty of literally dying in the arms of one's maker, and the ecstatic orgasm of becoming truly *alive* and drunk on the elixir of one's own transmogrified blood.

To a human with no such ambitions, perhaps no explanation is possible. But to any being who has suffered the rituals of transformation and awakened in an altered and infinite state of awareness, no further explanation is necessary.

I knew Atom wanted that state. And because of his own failure with Zen, he was highly motivated. For that reason alone, he would endure whatever I asked of him, whatever pain I might inflict on him.

That, too, was part of the unwritten contract between us.

He stood there next to my bed for a very long time, waiting, trembling, expecting.

"What do you want from me, Thorn?" he asked at last, his voice low and filled with need.

I looked him up and down very slowly, had him turn around and face the wall. I caressed the barely exposed globes of his rump so lightly he could barely feel it, yet he must certainly have craved it all the more because of its undelivered promise.

In the massive and ornate mirror, his manhood peeked out through the front of the robe. A sharp breath sounding like a wild wind came from his lips. His hand twitched, needing to go to the source of his pain.

Standing behind him, I pressed my lips to his neck. My fangs traced the artery in his neck.

But I did not satisfy him.

"Until the rituals are completed, you must not touch yourself, for that is a right you have surrendered to me alone. Do you understand?"

When he didn't immediately answer, I slipped an arm around his waist and grasped his abundant protrusion in my hand, squeezed it hard for emphasis until he drew a sharp intake of breath.

"Do you understand that I own you – and *this* – until such time as you own yourself, until such time as you are finally *free*?"

He groaned, the sound of an old house under the stress of a storm. His hips squirmed as he tried to thrust into my palm. I allowed him one single push, and then I removed my hand completely before he could even think of release. In his intense state of arousal, it wouldn't have taken much to bring him over the summit, but that was not a relief I intended to afford him – not yet.

"Disobey me – touch yourself, and I will know," I told

him, retracing the path in his neck, but now with just the tip of my tongue. "And you will be punished severely."

I wanted to torture him as Ambrose had tortured me. I wanted to make him suffer as Ambrose had caused me to suffer.

Atom trembled at my threats. "Please... don't. Don't ask me to make a promise you know I can't keep."

Of course, we both knew that was precisely the point.

When I bit him just short of drawing blood, his hand twitched, straying again toward the folds of the robe where his phallus was peeking out, screaming in shades of hot pink for deliverance.

Perhaps I would have taken pity on him and simply fucked him (as he so rudely liked to label the act) there on the floor of my bedchamber. No need to invoke the second phase of the ritual. Just a slow and easy fuck between consenting adult vampyres.

But even as the beast was citing the top ten reasons why it would have been a very bad idea under the circumstances – not the least of which was his argument that a period of enforced celibacy was the catalyst for awakening the dark desire which was the second gate – I became aware of an unusual light shining in through the north window.

PART TWO
The Inevitability of Change

CHAPTER SIX
The Parish of Mortality

Distracted as I was with Atom's carotid artery thrumming an invitation against my lips and the soft globes of his rump pressed against my thigh, it took a few moments and a conscious act of will before I was able to pull away from the demon, who made every attempt to prevent me from doing just that.

Finally pushing him roughly from me until he landed on his back on the bed, I hurried to the window to see what in all unspoken hells was creating such a cacophonous uproar of light in my world of cherished darkness.

At first, I could not believe what I was seeing. Far to the north, well beyond the silver-blue glow of the Foreboding Mountains, a pale yellow sun had risen and actually appeared to be moving across the sky the way the sun in the World Above rose and set. This, of course, was impossible in Umberlight, for even though Atom had dragged some fragment of Time in on his shoes, he did not possess the power to manifest even a very tiny sun.

The spray of light was isolated over a relatively small area and posed no serious threat to the four major regions of Umberlight, but the fact that it existed at all awakened an anger I had seldom felt.

If I had not summoned the sun, that left only one suspect. The fairies never strayed from their beloved forest, and the scarecrow had no will of his own.

I turned to Atom with a look that spoke my thoughts aloud before they ever left my lips. "What have you *done*?" I demanded, and moved toward him even as he was scrambling backward on the bed like some mutant crab attempting to evade a hungry predator.

"I *didn't*!" he wailed, sounding very much like an ornery boy caught masturbating in the choir loft. "I mean – maybe I *did*, but I didn't think it would actually *happen*!"

He was making no sense. Those who believe they are about to die seldom do.

He managed to skitter off the other side of the bed, and might have succeeded in escaping into the stairwell were it not for the fact that the massive wooden door slammed shut at the command of my will a split second before he reached it.

Because I did not need to navigate furniture or traverse the illusion of distance, I was on him an instant later, holding his smaller body flat against the door like an insect about to be pinned to a board. His eyes had gone wide. His erection had gone soft.

He was genuinely terrified.

"What have you *done*?" I repeated, compelling him with every gram of power I possessed to speak the truth before I killed him on the spot. He knew I could – for despite the fact that he was vampyre, he was also still somewhat human, with certain human frailties and vulnerabilities.

He choked back a cry of terror, then said in a very small voice, "Just let me explain?"

Over the centuries, I had come to loathe those words. Actions taken without thought always require some long-winded justification, and humans and immortals alike are perpetually standing in line to explain some absurd thing they have done which never would need explaining if only they had never done it in the first place.

"Speak!" I shouted, and showed him my fangs in a way that promised no mercy if I did not like what he had to say.

When he squirmed a little, I let him go and followed him

when he moved to the north window. He stood there silhouetted against the distant yellow glow.

"Son of a bitch," he muttered to himself.

"Well?" I prompted, impatient. "Do you intend to offer this explanation of yours, or should I terminate you and go back to bed?"

Now he turned toward me, and because I had come up so close behind him, we were almost chest to chest. He reached out and placed one hand over my heart as if physical contact might staunch my ire.

"It must've been the spiders," he stammered in a rapid-fire voice that was trying to say too much too fast and therefore not a single word of it was coherent. "Or maybe we really are on the shore leave planet from *Star Trek*. You know – where anything you think just pops up out of the ground but some of it bites you on the ass. Like when Rodriguez thought of the tiger—"

"Atom!" I interrupted, and shook him by the shoulders the way one might shake an hysterical person. "Just tell me what *happened*." I had no idea what he was talking about, of course. Certainly I knew nothing of Rodriguez or a tiger.

Taking a deep breath to center himself, he gave a curt nod as if finally hearing what I had said. Another breath that turned to fog in the cold wind blowing in from the north. And finally he managed to speak.

"You were out for a long time," he began. Then, seeing my confusion, he quickly added, "When you were in the River of Stars, I mean. It was a *long* time, Thorn."

I hadn't given it much thought, for time in Umberlight had become a matter of perspective. One either perceived it, or one chose *not* to perceive it.

"What does that have to do with the sun?" I asked, wondering if he were just making it up as he went along as a way to delay his own extermination.

He turned again toward the window, shifting from one foot to the other in a manner that bespoke anxiety.

"You need to see it in perspective, Thorn," he insisted. "I mean – we need to just *go* there so you can see it for yourself."

I fully intended to do just that, but not without more information first. "And what – *precisely* – is 'it' that you think I should see?"

He took a halting step back from me until he was butted up against the blue marble sill of the window. The fact that the arch-shaped opening had no glass or other safety features had never been of concern to me anymore than the realization that it was several hundred feet to the ground. For one who could essentially fly, there was no fear of falling.

Atom didn't seem to notice the danger he was in – or if he did, perhaps he considered it a merciful alternative to *my* wrath.

"It's the Parish of Mortality?" he said, but it came out as a question more than an answer.

"The what?"

"The Parish of Mortality?" he repeated, and now his voice was barely a whisper, dampened almost entirely by the cold wind that came in through the window, but which was not permitted to travel more than a few paces into the room.

That's what I thought he said. And it was anything *but* what I wanted to hear, for I could already surmise where this was going.

"Look, Thorn," he began to jabber in his own defense, "whether you like it or not, others *are* coming – other immortals, I mean. Other vampyres. And it's going to happen sooner than you think – it can't be avoided no matter *how* much you try to keep them out! The fireflies are just the first. You *have* to know others are coming! And not all of them are going to be as evolved as you are – *if* that's what you are! I mean – I didn't mean that like it came out. I mean–"

"What *do* you mean?" I interrupted when he stumbled over his flapping tongue. I already knew, but I wanted to hear him say it. I would *force* him to say it.

He ducked his head, didn't meet my eyes. "Some of them

like to feed," he mumbled apologetically. Then, looking up with that expression of defiance I'd come to expect, he added, "They're going to need a food source, goddammit!"

"And so you took it upon yourself to open a commissary for vampyres?" I said. "How very thoughtful of you."

"I – but – it isn't *like* that!" he stammered.

But it was *exactly* like that.

I turned away from Atom and went to sit in the plush chair next to the bed. My actions were calculated and precise, not at all random. I remained silent for some time, letting him fret while he stood there with his back to the window and snow blowing in to dust his shoulders. In the silk robe which was as thin as it was short, there was no doubt he was cold. I saw him shiver, pretended not to notice.

"Aren't you going to say anything?" he asked when the distant sun over the distant Parish of Mortality had completed three cycles.

"What would you have me say?" I asked rhetorically. "You have disobeyed the very first commandment I ever gave you – that you must never bring mortals into Umberlight."

He looked genuinely hurt for a moment, then went right back to trying to defend an action that could have no defense.

"This thing is a lot bigger than you think, Thorn," he argued, becoming adamant, close to belligerent. "Maybe you created this place, but you can't *own* it!"

He was perilously close to finding out exactly what I had meant when I had threatened him with punishment.

"It was never my intent to own it, Atom. I only wanted to live here in peace, away from the dis-ease of humanity." I paused to let that sink in, though I doubted it could penetrate his thick head. "And now you have made that impossible. You tell me *I* cannot own Umberlight, yet you come in as an unwelcome stranger and immediately begin behaving as if *you do*. Ironic, no?"

Observing his reaction, I began to realize that my words could hurt him far more than anything I might do to his body.

It was a bit of knowledge well worth having, though one I kept to myself for the time being.

"It wasn't like that," he said again, staring at the floor. His demeanor left no doubt as to his utter defeat. "But you'll believe whatever you want to believe, so maybe you should just kill me and get it over with."

He certainly could be a drama queen when it suited him.

"Very well," I agreed, standing up and moving toward him. "It does seem to be the only rational solution – for if I let you live, there is no way of knowing what *more* damage you will do."

His eyes widened and his knees went weak. I think he actually believed I would do it. And for that reason, perhaps it was no surprise when he stumbled backward and went tumbling out the window, plunging with a shrill scream toward his end.

CHAPTER SEVEN
A lovely evening for a stroll

In hindsight, I have wondered if the little bastard *knew* I would catch him, or if he only dared to *hope* I might. Whatever his agenda might have been, I did catch him and instead of landing at the base of the tower, we came to rest at the outermost edge of what Atom had called the Parish of Mortality. He was passed out from fright in my arms, but began to stir when I stood him on his feet and shook him by the back of the neck the way a mother tiger shakes an unruly cub.

"Wake up," I commanded, and held onto him for only as long as it took him to stand on his own.

For several minutes, Atom stood at my side in absolute silence. Finally, he asked the obvious. "Am I dead?"

I shot him a menacing look. "Not *quite* yet," I assured him.

When I say we stood there for several minutes, that's exactly what I meant. Here at the borderlands where the Parish of Mortality butted up against the northwestern range of the Foreboding Mountains, time was very much in attendance, and could be felt like a heavy gravity that was always hungry to pull every living thing back into the earth – an unrelenting force that digested mortals in his ravenous belly and finally spit them out as lifeless husks.

A peculiar silver fog seemed to form a transition zone between Umberlight and the newly manifested parish, and as I was beginning to discern, the mist was actually a perceptual barrier beyond which the inhabitants of the mortal settlement could not see or travel.

Though that was a somewhat comforting bit of knowledge, I could not decide whether to be sick or angry, and since neither would go even one step toward returning Umberlight to the state in which it had existed before the Parish of Mortality sprang into being, I chose to simply observe and gather information.

For all intents and purposes, the settlement appeared to stretch for several miles. Nondescript houses lined nondescript streets while nondescript people in nondescript attire went through the meaningless motions of their nondescript lives. In that way, it was no different from the World Above – which was apparently what Atom had wanted when he summoned the spiders to complete the basic structure of the parish. At least, that is what I concluded *must* have happened.

This addendum to Umberlight *had* to be from Atom's mind, because the houses were like nothing I had seen before (I would later discover the dwellings were called 'tract homes'), and filled with illumined gadgets and jabbering gizmos which could only be from some unfathomable future. In addition, the carriages in front of the mortal's warrens required no horses, and ran on nothing more than the turn of a magical key. Rain came *up* from the ground instead of down from the sky, though at some point I would later discover it wasn't rain at all, but something known as a sprinkler system for watering the grass. The windows were illumined from within, not by the glow of candles, but through some strange magic which Atom called electricity.

The sun rose and set while we remained there in the fog beyond the perceptual boundaries of the humans, neither of us speaking a single word for what must have been hours.

Finally I could no longer contain my curiosity. "Where did they come from?" I asked at last. There were families and couples and individuals, as varied as one would expect to find in any thriving city in the World Above.

Atom only shrugged. "All I know is that when I woke up by the river, all of this was already here – like I dreamed it."

"And you didn't think to tell me about it?"

He looked properly chagrinned, ducked his head, kicked at the dirt. "Do I *look* stupid?" But he decided not to wait for an answer when he saw the expression on my face. "No matter how it got here, I knew you'd be pissed off, and I knew you'd blame *me*, so I was hoping..."

His voice trailed off into the silence of the frigid air blowing down from the Foreboding Mountains at our backs – mountains which were visible to Atom and myself, but which the humans perceived as something entirely different, *if* they perceived them at all.

"You were hoping it would go away?" He was even more like a child than I had previously thought. I sighed heavily, exasperated.

I didn't like the fact that he was a lot more powerful than I had first believed – apparently powerful enough to manifest an entire settlement and fill it with mortals. But in direct contradiction, he was looking pale and weak, and perhaps a bit older than he had when he had first appeared next to me at the edge of the Firefly Forest. How long had it been? There was no way to know. A very long time that was no time at all.

But there was no denying that he was aging. Not rapidly. But he *was* aging.

Something inside me twisted and rebelled at that realization. I may not have been in love with Atom, but I did like him despite himself. I suppose I considered him a friend, had I been required to label the nature of our relationship – and it pained me to think I would not be able to save him. Even if I knew the secrets of becoming a Creator, I did not know if I had the raw and seemingly elusive *power*.

In one moment, I felt there was nothing I could not do. In the next moment, whatever it was that passed for reality would come crashing down around me and cause me to wonder how I could be so arrogant, even within the private confines of my own mind.

Some part of me that *wanted* to be gentle with him started to reach out. But the beast who had become my guide held my hand at my side, not allowing it to move.

"Until you are fully immortal, it is not safe for you here," I said instead. "The light of the sun generates time, you realize."

"I think of it more like a grow light for humans," Atom

said with a boyish grin.

"A grow light?" I repeated.

Atom looked at me the way one might study a bug.

"Damn, you need a software upgrade, dude," he said. "You'd still be a Connecticut Yankee in King Arthur's Court – well, kinda in reverse, I guess. But – *damn* – it's like talking to a caveman sometimes!"

I had no idea what he was talking about.

"Too bad it's not like *Star Trek*. Hell, I could just mind meld with you and bring you up to speed."

He did seem to have a deep investment in this thing he called *'Star Trek'*.

Without consciously realizing it, we had begun walking beyond the fog and into the suburbs of the parish itself. Though we should have stood out like proverbial elephants in the room, no one gave us a second look, even though my attire was not at all like theirs, and Atom's... well... Atom's attire revealed far more than most polite human beings would have wanted to see walking down a street in their civilized neighborhood.

"They probably just think you came from a costume party," Atom commented, sneaking a tendril into my mind to know what I was thinking.

"And you?" I wondered, looking pointedly at the robe which did not quite meet in the front.

He shrugged again. "Me? I'm just a temporal distortion to them."

I wasn't going to give him the satisfaction of admitting – again – that I had no idea what he was referring to.

He explained anyway. "This is the time I'm actually *from* – or at least the time I was in when I followed those silly fireflies into Umberlight," he clarified. "Long story short, you can't be in two places at once, so since I'm *here* with you, I can't be *here* with *them*, so if they see me at all, I'm just a trick of the light." He paused, furrowing his brows thoughtfully. "At least that's what I'm hoping for."

He was a good story-teller, even when he wasn't making sense. I just kept walking, curious where the road would lead, secretly enjoying the time of day when it had begun to turn from the long shadows of late afternoon into the mystical embrace of approaching dusk – the crack between the day and the night. While I would not admit it even to myself, I had missed certain aspects of the mortal world.

Though the climate in the nearby mountains was always well below freezing and perpetually shrouded in snow, the Parish of Mortality seemed to thrive on temperatures that varied only slightly, and were always just warm enough or just cool enough.

It was *pleasant*.

I could appreciate the tranquility of it, though I found myself increasingly disturbed by the droning prattle that poured out from every window of every front room, accompanied by a flickering blue glow emanating from some manner of thin rectangular box. Far more disturbing than the endless drone was the fact that every human appeared to be mesmerized by the mindless repetitions and the chorus of intermittent laughter coming from some audience not immediately apparent.

It was perplexing at best.

Seeing my reaction, Atom laughed out loud. "Television," he explained, as if that should mean anything. "Where I'm from, it's the control mechanism and the comfort food of choice for the whole population."

It was annoying that Atom knew so much about this dangerous parish while I knew so little. It *could* jeopardize the power I needed to maintain over him if I had any intention of holding up my end of the bargain to try to turn him. And it was a bargain I did intend to keep – not because I am always a man of my word, but because Atom had information I needed if I were to get my Emily back.

Emily.

In that moment, I was horrified to realize I could barely

recall her face, the color of her hair, the light in her eyes.

Things were happening too fast, and not at all as I had envisioned them. Even the beast had fallen silent, in awe of what we were both witnessing in a world that had once been so very simple and so very *empty*.

"Don't worry about it," Atom said as if to comfort me – an effort that was arrogantly presumptuous. "Before we go back to the farm, we'll snatch a laptop and you can learn all about the future – assuming it can connect to the internet from the tower, but I see no reason why it shouldn't. I mean – it's not like there's a *real* wi-fi signal down here, so if these bleating humans can get the net, the technology should work even if it *shouldn't* work, right?"

Atom could bequeath a headache to a stone boulder.

Then again...

I felt a deep rumble from somewhere in the center of my being – not unlike the purr of a large cat. And only in retrospect did I realize it was the contented laughter of the beast.

You said you want to play poker and influence the destiny of kings, that darker part of me said, clearly pleased with himself.

I don't understand. I was getting *very* tired of hearing those words, particularly from myself.

The explanation came not in language but in a rapid influx of images and explanatory word files which the beast referred to as a psychic download. It wasn't exactly painful, but it *was* disconcerting to feel both ignorant and omniscient in the same moment.

He needed to think it was his own idea, the darkling said, and I pictured some untamed aspect of myself casually sharpening his fangs as a prelude to the kill.

Are you saying he did <u>not</u> create this mortal ghetto?

He did not, the beast confirmed.

Then who did?

You did, of course. This was said with certainty and a fair amount of amusement.

And why would I do that? I asked myself. *And for that matter, __how__ would I have done it, since I have no knowledge of the trappings of the future?*

The beast was evasive but not without empathy for my pathetic ignorance. He spoke in short syllables, as if to a child – for which I might have dealt him a painful blow were it not for the fact that it would have landed on my own face.

You only __think__ you don't know these things – but the moment you breathed Umberlight into being, you stepped outside the pre-existing hologram and into quantum underpinnings of the infinite.

Okay, so maybe he *needed* to speak in short syllables as if to a child. I gave no response.

Put simply, just as Umberlight is evolving, so are you. So are __we__.

So now I was referring to myself as the royal 'we'.'

Clearly I needed a lot of therapy, even though it did not yet exist as such.

The spiders know you. You know Atom. And so the spiders know Atom as well as they know you, the beast explained as if it should have been obvious. *They may have taken what they needed from his mind, but they took the __power__ from you.*

In some corner of reality, perhaps that made perfect sense.

And what of Atom? I asked.

He is not what he seems, my darkling otherself reminded. *But for as long as he thinks he's in control, his pride will put him at a disadvantage and give control over to us.*

Control of __what__? I demanded, rapidly losing what little patience I may once have had.

Everything, the beast replied. *Everything you ever needed to know about the dayshine world you'll find on the internet.*

I found that hard to believe.

What day of the week was June 9, in the year 865? the beast asked in direct response to my skepticism.

Why should I know? Why would I __need__ to know? He was starting to irritate me almost as much as Atom.

It was a Saturday. You'd know if you had the internet, the fiend replied smugly. *And that is what Atom can give you if you play his game.*

Wonderful. I was about to become the proud owner of some manner of archaic calendar.

Anything else? I asked with no small amount of sarcasm.

You should fuck him once in awhile to keep him happy. A happy boy is an obedient boy.

I deserved that for talking to myself.

But for the moment, I let it go, having already discovered that this aspect of myself I had been calling 'the beast' was far more knowledgeable than the part of myself I had always known as Thorn. And while I did not fully comprehend everything he had said, I could feel the threads of it weaving a tapestry in some corner of my mind. I had to trust the process, even though trust was a commodity I did not give easily, even to myself.

When I looked up from my mental wanderings, darkness had fallen over the parish. We had walked together in silence for what might have been a kilometer in standard measure. What struck me as odd was that even though it was a magnificent evening, not a single person had come out for a stroll or to gaze up at the scintillating blanket of stars. In a world teeming with life, there was no *Life* at all.

With one exception that had the bad manners to startle me.

As we rounded a corner, I suddenly found myself face to face with a young man who appeared to be perhaps 25 years of age. To be truthful, I had become so absorbed in thought that I bumped squarely into him, the collision forceful enough to cause us both to stumble backward.

"I'm so sorry!" the man said, and placed a hand on my elbow to steady me. "Are you all right?"

Of course I was all right. I'm a vampyre. I should have been asking *him* that question, but I smiled politely and offered the typical response which would have been expected.

"No harm done, my lord. 'Tis a lovely evening for a stroll,

no?"

Atom winced and gave me a sharp elbow to the ribs. "You sound like you just got out of a geek speak symposium at a fucking ren faire!" he chastised, embarrassed at my manner of speech.

At this, the young man laughed, and it was clear he could not only see Atom, but also heard him just fine. So much for the anonymity of a temporal distortion. Atom looked crestfallen and more than a little uncomfortable. He tugged at the front of the robe, pulling it together, trying to yank it lower.

The stranger seemed not to care. And in all fairness, it was sufficiently dark underneath the sheltering trees that he may simply not have noticed.

"I went to a ren faire once," the young man revealed, completely at ease. "My boyfriend thought it would be a hoot, but he got all jealous and weird when one of the knights started hitting on me instead of him." He laughed again. "I dumped him right after that, so now I'm back to being solo."

He said this so casually I could scarcely believe what I was hearing. Was this total stranger admitting to being openly homosexual? Had the world changed so much in 345 years that one could speak freely of such things without fear of imprisonment or even execution?

Atom elbowed me hard in the ribs again – an offense for which I made a mental note to punish him severely later on. When he spoke, it was in a whisper so silent that only vampyre ears could have detected it.

"He thinks we're a gay couple." Then, seeming to reconsider his words, he said, "Homosexual. Queer. Tutti-fruity. Whatever word you use in caveman grunt-speak."

I understood him the first time. And so his insolence added another item to the rapidly growing list of offenses.

Focusing on the stranger, I returned his smile and held out one hand in the typical fashion. To touch him would reveal certain information. To drink of him would reveal far more. The fact that he was handsome and of a lean athletic build even made the prospect appealing, for it had been a very long time since I had fed, and though I did not require either blood or animus to survive, I was enough of a sensualist that I did not turn down an opportunity when it stumbled out of the night and landed in my arms.

"My name is Thorn, and this is Atom," I said by way of polite introduction.

The man accepted my hand and, as I had hoped, held it a few beats longer than social custom might have dictated. There was no denying he was attracted to me, which was my agenda.

"Jason," he said with what could only be interpreted as a warm invitation. "Jason Green."

Reluctantly, he drew his hand away and turned to Atom, repeating the peculiar human ritual of shaking hands and mumbling one's name. It was the kind of momentary distraction I needed.

As a skilled predator, it is my nature to take what I want in such a manner that the prey believes they walked into the trap of their own volition, and quite eagerly at that. When Jason took a step back from Atom and that awkward moment of social adjustment descended on him, I simply moved in, placing one hand on his hip, the other behind his head, my fingers tangling in the glossy brown hair that was cut into a fashionably ragged style and felt like liquid silk on my palm.

He drew a sharp breath, not of fear, but a little gasp of desire that swept over him when I pulled him to me and kissed him with great force. With no hesitation whatsoever – perhaps because I had commandeered the element of total surprise – his lips opened to me and our tongues met in an intense battle that went on until he surrendered to me completely and his head fell back to reveal the thrumming artery in his neck.

To do this thing properly is an art – an exchange between two beings, one whose nature is to take and the other whose

100

nature it is to give.

While Atom looked on and mumbled "Jesus H. Christ," no less than three times under his breath, I cut with as much tenderness as I could into Jason's neck with the tips of my fangs.

And while I have told you I do not need human blood for survival, I have never said I do not enjoy imbibing that dark elixir when circumstances demand it and when my victim is not a victim at all, but has become a willing participant in the dance.

And so I drank, taking the warm essence of him into my preternatural body until his sharpest memories and deepest thoughts wound their way through my veins and began delivering up their secrets. Even as I was becoming intoxicated on this mortal, I realized once more that I *should* have been able to glean similar knowledge from Atom when I drank from him, but where the sharp colors of Life should have come bursting onto my tongue, there had been only the carnal heat of carnal heat itself. I had no explanation, though I fully intended to seek one.

Later.

But for that moment, as I floated in the illumined sea of animus carried in Jason's blood, little else mattered.

It is impossible to describe the experience of feeding just as it is impossible to describe the sensation of a sexual climax to someone who has never experienced it.

I indulged myself utterly, while Jason clung to me as a lover would, and made contented little whimperings that were more accurately offerings of gratitude.

I was often humbled by mortals, particularly those who could give themselves over to this thing so easily, so willingly. It would not have played out any differently had I never compelled him to compliance. He *wanted* it. And because he wanted it, I could deny him nothing.

The taste of his blood was unusually sharp, like a copper penny warmed in the summer sun. The taste of his lifeforce was contrastingly sweet, reminiscent of a ripe mandarin orange.

I learned form Jason that the humans called the settlement Tempest – named for the mysterious undulating fog which hung heavily in the air around the outskirts of the city and had never been scientifically explained to anyone's satisfaction. I also learned that they perceived their town to be a thriving suburb of Los Angeles. To Jason's perceptions, he was simply a man in an ordinary town somewhere on a planet known as Earth, circling a yellow sun in the year 2015.

He had no concept of the fact that he was actually in a world that was not really Earth at all, but a construct of thought and energy cobbled together by a disgruntled vampyre sometime in the late 17th century.

Perception is reality.

Even if I had thought to reveal the truth to Jason, he would not have believed me. He *could* not have believed me, for the narrative he had woven for himself told him his beliefs were true, even though they were nothing more than a convenient back story.

Like most humans, he was an actor in a play that was no more real than a Shakespearean comedy.

There was so much more I wanted to learn from him, but when I had taken enough to fill not only my curiosity but also a hunger I had thought I no longer possessed, I withdrew my fangs from his neck and took a moment to center myself back in my own unique identity.

Realizing after a moment that Atom was staring at me with what could only be labeled as human jealousy, I remembered that he had not fed since his arrival in Umberlight.

"Are you hungry?" I asked.

He nodded, making no attempt to disguise his need.

I motioned him to me, and continued to hold the semi-conscious man in such a way that presented his throat to the imp.

"Be gentle with him," I cautioned.

Atom did as he was instructed, meeting my eyes for a moment as if asking one last time for permission, then at my nod lowering his mouth to the two small punctures left by my bite. He moaned softly as he drew the essence of this man into his mouth, and I could not help but notice that he became spontaneously erect, his abundant phallus pushing the front of his robe open even as he struggled to keep his hand from straying to soothe that needful burn.

It cannot be denied that watching him drink was sensual and alluring. And though I might have preferred to deny my arousal, it became difficult to ignore when my erection began pressing against the tight confines of my leggings.

In the position I was in – holding Jason upright to keep him from falling while Atom drank his fill – it was also impossible to prevent my hardness from nudging against the warmth of the human's thigh.

Feeling that pressure and clearly being experienced with *precisely* what it was, the stranger stirred in my embrace, and even managed to lift his head a little, his clear blue eyes opening as he whispered, "Let me. *Please*. Let me!" And in his mind, he whispered with awe, *Is it you? Can it really be you?*

Though I did not know specifically what he was referring to, to be wanted so deeply by a human is intrinsic to what it means to be a vampyre. I could feel his desire as if it were my own, for it had *become* my own. ,

I was drunk on him.

With his blood flowing wildly through my veins, there could be no mistaking his intent. And though I might have considered myself an extremely private man with no exploitable vices, I could not deny that I *ached* to feel his warm, wet lips on me every bit as much as he wanted to take me into his mouth.

The symbiosis was preordained by Nature herself.

Tangling my fingers in Atom's hair, I lifted his head away before he could take more than Jason could give. They both moaned with disappointment at being parted, though Atom managed to remain on his feet even as the other man went weak and I lowered him to his knees there on the sidewalk beneath the sheltering oaks somewhere in the heart of Tempest.

Atom started to speak – undoubtedly to protest being left out – but I met his gaze with a stern look. "You will watch," I instructed him, becoming more skilled than I might have thought in the art of brutality. "You will not speak. You will not climax."

"I – but –"

"Be *silent*!" I commanded, though in truth I could barely speak at all, for Jason was a skilled predator in his own right, and had quickly pulled the front of my leggings down in such a way that my phallus sprang free and bobbed heavily in the loving embrace of the warm night air.

A moment later, he had taken the head in his mouth and began a religious ministry that one might have expected from an experienced nymph. His tongue was hot and unrelenting, his lips suckling as a hungry infant might suckle its mother's breast. He clung to my hips and encouraged me to push deeper into his mouth, and because I have already confessed that I could deny him nothing, I was compelled to comply.

I cannot say how long this continued. I only know that I became lost in the artful manipulations he lavished on me, until I had become nothing more than a pinpoint of awareness centered at the swollen tip of my hardness. When he knew I was near to climax, he slipped one hand underneath the shaft to cup the twin mounds of my balls, squeezing gently until I grasped the back of his head and thrust deep into his welcoming throat.

The force of it was indescribable when it came, when the energetic rush of my animus spilled into his mouth. He swallowed eagerly – *hungrily* – suckling harder and harder until I was certain I would turn wrong side out or disintegrate completely.

Then, finally, when I was more satisfied than I could recall being in a very long time, he lifted his head away with a sharp gasp of sheer pleasure.

"My prince," he whispered, close to weeping. "My *prince!*"

People say the most peculiar things in the throes of sexual delirium. I thought little of it at the time, though in reality, *I* should have been the one crying out in awe. But as I stood there – barely *able* to stand – I realized just how much I had missed the adoration of mortals.

Feeling a great sense of gratitude and respect for Jason, I knelt at his side and once again lowered my mouth to his neck. The tiny puncture wounds were still bleeding a little, and so I tongued them closed and healed them with a kiss that lingered a bit longer than was necessary, but not nearly as long as I would have liked.

Jason was, in a single word, exquisite.

And yet…

It was my nature to fall in love with humans the same way small boys fall in love with a puppy. The love was real, but far too often it was transitory and of a somewhat shallow nature. I loved the taste of them. The flavor of their lives. The comedies and tragedies they carried in their veins, sweet as raw honey. Nevertheless, I could count on one hand the times in my very long life that I had been *truly* in love with a human, and perhaps because each of those loves had ended tragically (for they could end no other way) I had learned never to love too deeply, and always to return the puppy to its rightful home before becoming too attached.

And so I whisked Jason back to his nondescript tract home on his ordinary street, and left him sleeping peacefully in his bed with the beige sheets and the big screen TV mumbling softly to itself on the dresser.

His blood was in my veins now, just as my animus was in his belly, seeding his mind with visions as he slept. In that way, we would never truly be parted again, and should I ever need an ally for any reason, I had only to open my eyes inside his mind to know precisely where he was at any given moment. If he remembered anything at all of our encounter, it would be a hazy half-memory of what might have been a dream.

I turned to leave, but my eye caught something on the nightstand next to Jason's bed. While it looked more like some odd manner of shiny notebook, it came to me through the blood-bond I now shared with Jason that this was the thing Atom had referred to as a 'laptop'.

Though I am not normally a thief, I snatched it up and shoved it inside the folds of my shirt. Then like the moon embraced by clouds, I was gone.

CHAPTER EIGHT
The vampyre cathedral

When I returned to where I had abandoned Atom on a street corner, it was to find him sitting underneath a large tree in the dark with his knees drawn up to his chest and his chin resting on one leg. To say he was a forlorn portrait of neglect would have been an understatement.

I wasn't born last night, of course.

I saw the ploy for what it was. He was hurt. He was jealous. He was angry.

All of which were part of the plan the beast had been whispering into my ear since our arrival in Tempest.

There was nothing to be said, so I merely motioned him to his feet. I had seen more than enough of the Parish of Mortality. And to be candid, even my substantial energy reserves had been drained by Jason's considerable talent. Plus, the device I now concealed inside my shirt was more than a little intriguing. I was eager to learn of the future – if, indeed, such tall tales held any truth whatsoever.

My agenda was starting to seem within my reach.

"Come, Atom," I said sternly. "It's time we returned, and long *past* the time for you to show me the pathways back to my Emily."

Atom only stared at me, though he did scramble to his feet with an expression which could only be described as absolute outrage.

"Bullshit," he muttered under his breath. "You are so fucking *full* of bullshit!"

While his outburst surprised me, I could not help but laugh, which only incensed him all the more, of course.

"My, my," I commented with a chuckle. "Your behavior is worthy of a nagging wife. Did we get married somewhere along the way and I simply forgot?"

"Who are you trying to kid?" he demanded, the words tumbling out like a white-hot avalanche. "I just watched you kiss that guy like I have *never* been kissed, then he gave you a blow job that could have sucked the chrome off a trailer hitch, and you're going to stand there like some self-righteous straight asshat and tell me you want to go back to a *woman*? Who the fuck are you *kidding*?" he repeated.

"I owe you no explanation," I reminded him. "And you *will* do as I say or our arrangement will be considered null and void."

His eyes had turned to cat's eyes – almond-shaped and filled with heat. He opened his mouth to speak.

"Not. One. Word."

"But—"

That was one too many.

I turned away from him and, slamming a heavy door down between us, moved down a street we had not yet walked. I did not look back even when he hurried to catch up and began shuffling along several steps behind me.

He did not speak. Or if he did, I could not hear him through the barriers I had purposefully erected.

In reality, I was neither angry with him nor did I have any intention of abrogating our agreement. I wanted him to feel the sting of his disobedience – and ignoring him was the most effective way I had found to accomplish precisely that.

He would not run away, for he had nowhere to go. So all he could do was follow meekly and in blessed silence.

The entire settlement appeared to be laid out in logical patterns. Whereas the uninhabited cities and mystical settlements of Umberlight might follow the course of a winding stream or appear in clearings in the forest or nuzzle in around the foothills of a mountain range, these 'suburbs' as Atom called them, were designed with great precision – with every detail to practicality and not a single thought to aesthetics.

Store fronts and other establishments of use to mortals had been gathered together in a tidy cluster known as the business district. Schools to insure proper indoctrination into the prevailing belief systems were conveniently located at regular intervals, and had I not been informed otherwise, I might have deemed them to be prisons, for they were surrounded by fences and block walls even though there were no natural predators whom these humans might need to fear.

In brightly illumined windows, long-haired cats sat preening themselves after their evening meal, while their canine counterparts meditated on front porch steps or slept in well-tended yards of thick grass. A mockingbird talked to herself from atop a streetlamp that had flickered to light as if by magic, and a hum of cricket song filled the air with life.

Life.

In many ways, it was no surprise that humans were largely lazy creatures content to suckle at the teat of modern convenience, whether in my own time or in Atom's strange future. The comforts *were* comforting, and yet they were also deceptively transient. A moment of happiness in the arms of a beloved could not replace a lifetime of grief when that loved one was dead – a secret known mostly to vampyres, and to the restless few who traded in their comfortable sofas for a good pair of shoes and struck out alone on the road to freedom from the chains of the mundane.

Where that road might lead, one never knew. For me, it had led to Ambrose and the ironically dark blessing of immortality. For others, perhaps it led to some inner peace and a complete willingness to live and die as humans had lived and died since the beginning of time.

I had become so deep in thought that I scarcely noticed how far we had walked. Throughout the journey, Atom kept his head down and his hands behind his back. But when I glanced up from my contemplation and saw that the horizon was beginning to shimmer with shades of pink and orange and blue, I realized the night was done and soon the humans would begin skittering about on their way to work or school or appointments with doctors and lawyers, or whatever people do that goes to make up a life.

The fact that it was entirely illusion here in the larger womb of Umberlight mattered not in the least – and for the same reasons it didn't matter that it was all equally illusory in the World Above. The things humans believed were usually the things that had absolutely no meaning whatsoever – ideas strung together like bright little beads in the absurd hope of bringing order to chaos.

Not wanting to participate or even observe these ordinary machinations of these ordinary people, I motioned Atom to my side, preparing to will us back to the sanctuary of the tower. But as I came to an intersection where one gray street bled seamlessly into another, I was more than a little perplexed at what I saw rising out of the dense morning fog in front of me.

Though the houses and the people who lived in them have already been defined as mundane and uninteresting, the same could not be said of the massive cathedral that had sprung up out of the ground like some miscreant edifice of stone and stained glass. It stood in the center of a pristinely landscaped town square, where rows of roses lined the perimeter and perfumed the air with a scent of pink ambrosia.

I was sufficiently dismayed that I spoke out loud before I could pull the words back. "As if Time were not enough, they have brought their impotent God with them as well."

Atom looked at me as if I had gone daft. "You really don't get it, do you?" he said, breaking his silence with a tone that clearly bespoke his impatience with me. "That cathedral isn't a monument to God, Thorn. It's a monument to *you* – or, I should say it's a monument to us, to immortals, vampyres, whatever. These people aren't here because they think they've found heaven or because they're running from hell. They want to live forever, and to their way of looking at it, *you* are the only one who can give them that possibility!"

"As usual, you are making no sense whatsoever," I said calmly, though I was far from calm inside. "In one breath, you say the cathedral is a monument to immortals. In the very next breath, you say *I* am the central focus. Which is it?"

Atom stared at me as if trying to manufacture a safe answer that would not result in his immediate extinction.

"I don't know how to explain it in words you're going to understand," he said at last, which was *not* a safe answer. Seeing my expression, he hurried on. "I mean – look – it's like this – from what I can tell, the people here came from Earth. But they're the ones who saw through the bullshit – well, sort of anyway. But maybe they didn't see far *enough*, so they *know* there's something more to life than growing old and dying, but they don't know how to make that transition, so... well... I guess you could say they need a guru and you got the job."

He spoke so quickly that it didn't occur to me to ask how he knew these things.

I was horrified, for one thing was certain. "Then the fools have only traded one fairy tale for another!"

Atom wasn't so sure. "Even if God is a myth, *you* are not."

"What are you suggesting? Do you mean to say I should bring each of the trembling fools to my breast and attempt to transform them, when the truth is that I don't have any such ability, and they are mortal because they do not – *cannot* –even begin to let go of their false beliefs long enough to embrace their infinite potential?"

Atom laughed at me. "*That's* why they built the cathedral – to drag you out of hiding and get you to remind them of who and what they are. That little bit of shit you just rattled off is probably a *lot* more than they've ever gotten from all those new age self help mumbo jumbo steaming mountains of bullshit books they all illegally download in the hope of finding one single bit of real substance!"

His words made little sense, but I was getting used to that. "*I can't save them!*" I said with great emphasis. I was far too dismayed to say anything more.

Atom only shrugged – a habit he indulged often, a gesture of dismissal. "Maybe. Maybe not. But they need to believe in *something*, and here in Umberlight, *you* are the only god they know or want to know."

"But how can they know me at all?" I insisted, more rational than I ever wanted to be. In *my* world and time, vampyres were dismissed as myth, consigned to the realms of horror and fantasy. Unreal.

Atom was thoughtful for a moment, kicking at the nondescript colorless pavement. "Remember when I said there are legends about you even in my time?"

I did not *want* to remember, but I did. "And?"

He gave an ironic smile that was captured in the first dim glow of the rising sun. "I don't know how or even when it happened, but some of your journals were found and somebody decided to publish them." He paused, then haltingly added, "That's how I found you."

That gave me pause.

At first, I could see no reason why my private journals would cause anyone to mistake me for some wayward deity capable of handing out salvation for the asking, but humans as a species had never been particularly rational beings. And the things I had written in my journals *could* lead them to believe that the only requirement for becoming immortal was to meet a vampyre, share a kiss of blood, and wake up in a perfected vessel of pure energy, feeling refreshed and renewed and ready to take on the world.

It was a naive assumption, but perhaps not an unexpected one. Atom had once said that tales of vampyres had become prominent in his time and were even considered "all the rage" (his words) in the culture of his day. And while I had dismissed his ramblings as yet one more attempt to flatter me, I now began to wonder.

But it wasn't *only* that which might have caused the uproar. My journals also contained lengthy descriptions of the true nature of carnal pleasure, descriptions of what is possible when two beings surrender to their sensual power instead of hiding behind some quasi-religious fear that one will go blind or grow hair on one's palms if one indulges those basic drives

112

which are, in essence, the motivating catalyst behind the creation of Life itself – whether the sperm and egg of mortal life, or the primal elements of brutality, dark desire, and love which go into the creation of an immortal.

If the humans wanted to misconstrue what I had written, they were certainly capable. In fact, they could probably be *depended* upon to do exactly that.

I had to force myself to really *look* at the massive building. The cathedral itself was built of stone and crude mortar, but the stained glass windows were artistically phenomenal. Whereas similar windows in more conventional churches might depict the stations of the cross or the works of the saints, here they told a far different kind of story.

In one pane, a beautiful woman was accepting communion – not from a goblet filled with grape juice and hollow symbolism, but from the torn wrist of a vampyre "priest" who wore clothing similar to my own, and who also bore an uncanny resemblance to my own reflection.

In another window, this same dark doppelganger was seated on a river bank beneath a full moon, with the lifeless figure of a man cradled in his arms. Again, the vampyre's wrist was torn, and a single drop of silver was suspended in the space between immortal wrist and human lips. Above the intricate glass rendering was an inscription which read, "The prince cures the dead with the gift of anima."

I became so sickly mesmerized with looking at these ten-foot tall windows – all of which held some depiction of myself engaged in some unholy act with a mortal – that I scarcely noticed when the sun came crawling over the tallest peaks of the Foreboding Mountains. All together, there must have been twenty such renderings, and though I wanted nothing more than to deny what I was seeing, there could be no mistaking the fact that these humans of Tempest had learned not only of my existence, but also believed me to be capable of granting them immortality through their dreams or what they referred to as 'holy visions'.

As I had protested to Atom, they had only traded one absurd belief system for another, and the truly sickening thing was that the two weren't that different from one another after all. Whether the blood of Christ or the animus of the vampyre, the humans were looking for salvation *outside* of themselves, as had always been the case.

I could not speak. I did not *dare* speak, for I would have wailed like some rabid wolf and torn their cathedral to the ground. And while it would have done them all a favor, there was a part of me that whispered there *could* be some unforeseen advantage at some point later on to having this kind of power.

It was not a thought I wanted to own, for I had never been the kind of man who craved power over others. And yet... the beast pointed out in calm and rational terms that if I *really* wanted to be a Creator, that kind of power was not only necessary, but entirely unavoidable.

It also explained something Jason had said. He had cried out, *'My prince!'* And his innermost thoughts had wondered, *'Is it you? Can it really be you?'*

I did not want to consider the implications, for I certainly did not want to be anyone's prince and I *could* not be anyone's salvation.

Feeling the sun on my back at last, I glanced up from my mortified stupor to find Atom waiting patiently in the shade of a large oak in the center of the cathedral's courtyard. Like myself, he was in no real danger from the sun, but also like myself it was his nature to prefer the night and the company of sentient shadows.

He looked up when I approached him, and I could only describe his expression as one of genuine empathy. This petulant imp who could drive me mad actually felt sorry for me, for surely he must have sensed the profound impotence I felt when I realized how very much these humans *wanted* what they thought of as salvation and how completely incapable I was of even beginning to explain to them that any such deliverance from their mortality was in *their* power, and nowhere else.

And yet... was even *that* just another false belief system? Even I had not attained immortality alone. I had done the rituals and exerted the force of Will that had eventually led me to Ambrose. After finding him I had willingly endured the torments and unspeakable ceremonies required to transform me forever. It was not something given for the asking. It was not something one might wish and then idly wait for it to happen. It was the soul's *work* – and it did not always succeed, as Atom had discovered after engaging his own Otherself for twenty years only to fail miserably in his attempts to create his own immortality without any outside assistance.

Were these desperate, frightened humans any more insane than either of us?

I wanted to run. I wanted to scream. But there was nowhere to run and only the stained glass vampyre angels to hear my scream. The rest of the mortal world was huddled safely inside their beige and gray houses, drunk on the elixir that flowed from the glowing box. Indeed, *that* seemed to be the only god they would ever truly need or ever truly worship.

And yet, when I was able to retreat to a silent corner of my mind, I discovered what I had already concluded long ago.

No matter what the time period, no matter what evidence humans might possess which could prove to them that they alone – *each and every one of them* – were the most powerful being in the universe, they would always look for ways to abdicate their own power, ignore their own abilities and completely surrender their very lives to the mercy of imaginary gods and devils.

They would even build cathedrals to a vampyre.

The mortal world was a madhouse. And the lunatics had commandeered the asylum.

CHAPTER NINE
Home

We returned to the tower the same way we had traveled to the Parish of Mortality. I simply grabbed Atom by the hand and willed us to be in the sane sanctuary of my bedchamber. When we appeared there, I considered sending him to his room to consider the damage he had done, but if the beast within me was right – and I had no reason to believe otherwise – it wasn't Atom who had done the damage, but myself.

And yet, try as I might, I could not fathom *why* I had summoned the human settlement into existence, *if* indeed I had done it at all. The very thing I had created Umberlight to be rid of – Death itself – was now alive and well in what amounted to a suburb of my otherwise perfect world. There was simply no rational reason for *me* to have put it there.

Of course, Umberlight is forever evolving.

And of course, I have never been a lover of change, so perhaps it stands to reason I created the paradox by incessantly longing for the unchangeable while also longing equally to manifest the unthinkable (which is the very definition of change).

So another thing that took me by surprise upon returning to Smoketree Farm was the observation that a tremendous library had manifested not only in my private chamber, but throughout the many rooms and hallways and staircases of the massive stone tower. In my bedchamber alone, shelves of cedar stretched from floor to ceiling.

The books themselves ranged from very old leather-bound volumes to what Atom defined as "mass-market paperbacks." Arranged with great precision and obvious care, they created a sense of comfort, even an irrational sense of belonging, filling the air with a pleasant scent of ink and old paper.

A volume of ancient Greek poetry lay open at the foot of

the bed and, curious, I picked it up and read a page which was obviously much-beloved with ragged edges and dog-eared corners.

I, too, wish to sing of heroic deeds
(about the Atreides, and about Kadmus),
but the lyre's strings
can only produce sounds of love.
Recently, I changed the strings,
and then the lyre itself,
and tried to sing of the feats of Hercules,
but still the lyre kept singing songs of love.
So, fare well, you heroes!
because my lyre sings only songs of love.

I recognized the words from Anacreon, whom Ambrose had often quoted when he was drunk on wine from the vineyards or blood from the veins of humans. He may well have been a tyrant, but he had also been a lover of classical literature, and for that I had secretly admired him even while despising him equally.

Running my fingers over the fragile paper, inhaling the intoxicating aroma of its poetry, I took a moment to remember how much I have always loved the company of books. I had never thought to own so many for the simple reason that it is not my nature to stay in one place too long, and for a being who must occasionally steal away in the night with only the clothing on his back, it would not have been practical to be a collector of books.

And yet... perhaps for the first time, as I stood there in the silent and wondrous warmth of that embracing library, it began to sink in to me that Umberlight was now my *home*. Despite the recent discoveries, even despite the humans themselves, it was a place I had called into being and a place that would call me back whenever I might wander or stray into the World Above, or into any of the countless otherworlds waiting to be explored along the undiscovered pathways of the Ever-Forking Road or out in the vast unknown of the River of Stars.

I had lived in dozens – *hundreds* – of places since fleeing my Creator's estate sometime in the late 9th century, but I had never really had what amounted to a home.

The thought was both comforting and disturbing – another paradox, but one I chose not to explore at that particular moment. Whether I wanted to admit it or not, I was overwhelmed – a sensation to which I was not at all accustomed. And so I focused instead on what appeared to be real, rather than the endless implications skittering around in my mind.

Next to the bed and overlooking the west window, an imposing cherry wood desk had manifested, complete with a locking roll-top and a hutch which was likewise filled with books. Most were a complete mystery to me, and nearly all appeared to be manuals on how to navigate something called Windows 8 – an observation I found foreboding.

Taking the stolen laptop from my shirt, I placed it on the desk, though I had no idea how to access its alleged wisdom.

Atom had been peering over my shoulder, and seeing my confusion, he opened the lid of the thing the way one might open a coffin lid, then pressed some button that caused its rectangular glass mirror to flicker to life.

For a moment, he seemed unsure of himself, looking up at me as if for permission. "You want me to set it up for you?" he asked at last.

I didn't have much alternative. "Yes. Thank you."

He slid into the chair at the desk and began poking at the keyboard, and with every stroke some variation would appear on the top half of the gadget, which he said was known as the monitor and was not really a mirror at all.

In my defense, I am a fast learner, and I had also gleaned more information from Jason than I could have expected, so while I might have otherwise succumbed to a sense of panic that often accompanies great change, I felt instead a genuine curiosity where this odd device was concerned.

While Atom continued to fiddle, I returned to the north window, my mind still reeling over what I had discovered at the heart of the City of Tempest. Was such a thing even possible? And yet, I had seen it with my own eyes.

In the distance, the human settlement glowed like a bright tumor on the horizon, a living home for Death himself, a now ever-present reminder that my sanctuary was no longer mine alone, nor was it even a speak-easy for select immortals who might wander in from the World Above.

That, too, began to fully sink in.

Before returning to the tower, I had walked the entire perimeter of the cathedral, and had discovered behind it a large cemetery with very old headstones and very new ones alike. And while there had been no crosses or other typically religious markers, one grave, clearly a child's, bore an epitaph which read...

Prince of Angels
Kiss this Child With Life

That was when I grabbed Atom and fled through the quantum structure of time and space, back to my world where I was simply Thorn, and not some quasi-religious icon whom these intruding humans believed might save them from themselves in the same way they had relinquished that responsibility to gods or goddesses or some notion of a giant eagle or a sentient potato.

I could not even begin to digest the irony. What every immortal knew – or at least every vampyre who had survived the transformation – was that the thing which awakened one from the dead wasn't faith or belief or hope or even the magical elixir of the Creator's blood. What awakened one to immortality was the Will to *be* immortal – the steely determination to defy Death, the confidence to abandon time, and as Ambrose had finally confessed when I took my first immortal breath, what *really* gave a vampyre eternal life was the unparalleled *hunger* for Life itself.

"*Live!*" my Creator had commanded me as I was suspended between the obliterating dark and the infinite night, when my blood was pounding through his veins and he was bleeding it back to me from his firm male breast. "Live because you *can* and because it is *your* Will alone!"

No being could grant immortality to one who had moved through life as the walking dead the way most humans did. If life had *any* meaning at all, I had found it to be only one thing: life was the canvas and the arena for an individual's personal evolution. And those who did not evolve simply died, and that was all there was to it. Live forever or die trying. There was no middle ground, and even if I *had* the power to turn them, they would have been nothing more than empty vessels, mindless halflings once called revenants in works of garish fiction.

I could even begin to see how the typical myths and legends of vampyres had arisen. The unending thirst (though the reality was that it was a thirst for *Life*). The hatred of crosses or any other religious icon (though it was really a hatred of imprisonment by false belief systems). The idea that immortals cast no reflection (when the reality is that our reflections are far *brighter* than the human eye can perceive). The belief that sunlight was lethal to vampyres (when it was more accurately the darkness of *ignorance* that was lethal to *humans*).

I still had no idea where garlic came into it, but some things are best left a mystery.

"You're upset," Atom said, stating the obvious, but obviously doing it as an attempt to draw me out of my brooding contemplation.

He must have concluded his task, for he was standing at my back, following my gaze beyond the window. Beneath us, Smoketree Farm was cloaked in the ebony veil of night. The snow had stopped, leaving uncut jack o'lanterns wearing crowns of icy white, and every picket of the endless fence topped with the thick frosting of the storm.

In the distance, the scarecrow was stirring, summoning the wind back to the windmills and lighting a campfire in the east just to generate a scent of winter-pine on the breeze, a glimmer of pallid smoke against dark sky.

This was the home I had envisioned. *This* was where I belonged.

And yet... with the coming of the Parish of Mortality and especially the presence of the cathedral, everything I had come to love about Umberlight seemed to be fading – a song in the air, too quickly over; a crystal icicle, too rapidly melting.

The pain of it was almost more than I could bear.

I didn't turn to look at Atom, content to gaze out at the night instead. I was struggling to block out the Parish of Mortality altogether. Even though their pale sun continued to rise and set, I chose not to notice, moving abruptly from the north to the east window and turning my back on them the same way God must have turned his back on humanity.

A very long time passed. Days? Weeks? Years?

"Thorn?"

Atom's voice was soft-spoken and held genuine concern.

Perhaps he realized what I myself had not noticed. I was weeping, silver tears of animus dropping soundlessly onto the window sill where I had remained for longer than was healthy even for an immortal. If pressed, I could not have given a rational reason as to *why* I was crying, nor do I believe one always needs a reason.

With an effort, I brought myself under control, brushed my tears away with the back of my hand, and finally turned toward him. It was time to proceed with my own agendas – and what I wanted more than anything was to hold Emily in my arms and make love to her and give her the kiss of eternity so that we would never be parted again. I wanted to marry her in the blood with vows that did not include the words, 'Till death do us part.'

I wanted things to be as they once *were*. I wanted time to stop. I wanted love to last forever instead of disappearing like a ghost of fog on a far-off horizon. I wanted to *be* a Creator so I would no longer be such a disappointment to others – but, most of all, so I would no longer be such a disappointment to *myself*.

I made no move toward Atom. I simply said, "It's time you told me how to return to the World Above within the lifetime of the woman I loved."

A beat of silence. Then, barely a whisper: "So... you still intend to turn me?"

The need expressed in those words was more than the words themselves could express. The fact that I had once felt such need myself did nothing to soothe the ache that had moved in to inhabit my soul. Every living thing *wanted* something, and they all wanted far more than was mine to give.

A great and immovable burden had settled on my shoulders. Had my own cruel maker felt the same when I had stalked him in dreams and eventually found my way to him on that dark street? Was I just another needy pupil begging for deliverance from death?

"It is my *intent*, Atom," I said. "But I am not yet a Creator."

To my surprise, and perhaps to his own peril, he reached out and placed one hand in the middle of my back – a gesture that was surprisingly supportive and gentle, considering how I had treated him, considering how I *had* to treat him if I were to have any hope of honoring our agreement.

"I think you *are*," he said, not in any argumentative fashion, just as a statement of his sincere beliefs.

And though I must admit that his confidence in me did serve to bolster my confidence in myself, I could not depend on Atom's beliefs alone. I could not even depend on my own. Not when so much was at stake.

"How is it done?" I asked very directly.

Atom was silent for several minutes while I listened to the

approach of a new storm blowing in from the east – no doubt the scarecrow's offering in an effort to calm me. Lightning fractured the sky in the distance, followed by thunder still too far away to hear.

It was a comfort, though a small one. My heart was made of storms, my soul an unfinished poem.

I did not belong *anywhere*.

I waited.

"I can't tell you, but I can send you there - if that's what you really want," Atom said at last, though I could feel his disappointment, a sense of lost hope that was like a flower crushed under a runaway carriage.

Not wanting me to see him naked in that way, he forced a little chuckle and added, "You already know the way back. I mean... you've had the ruby slippers all along, so when you want to come home just click your heels together and say 'There's no place like home.'"

I had given up any expectation of a straightforward answer.

"Speak plainly," I demanded. "I am weary of riddles."

He looked momentarily hurt, but he didn't press it. "Mushrooms," he said.

"Mushrooms?"

"I saw some growing down by the river."

"The scarecrow began cultivating them at the same time he planted the pumpkin fields," I recalled.

"Have you ever eaten them?" Atom asked.

I decided to be honest with him, since he was going out of his way to be something other than obnoxious. "When I was a mortal, my Creator gave them to me once."

"And?" Atom prompted.

Though it had been over eight hundred years, I remembered it as if it were only a moonrise ago. "I saw the world as it is, and the worlds only sorcerers see for what they can be."

"Did you see the grid?"

Atom clearly had some knowledge of the mushroom's inner eye. "Yes." I paused, then realized he might be probing for information. "And you?"

He nodded. "A series of glowing green lines extended into infinity," he confirmed.

It was precisely what I had seen. At least it told me he was telling the truth – or perhaps he had only been ice fishing in my mind again.

"What does this have to do with the World Above?" I asked.

He grinned. "Those grid lines are pathways in *time*," he said, and though I could not begin to explain it, his words resonated with a truth that could not be denied. "They all overlap and flow together, but each one goes to a different place and a different time. So if you want to hook up with this Emily again, it's just a matter of taking the right road."

This seemed much easier to *say* than it might be to *do*. And there was no denying that Atom enjoyed knowing more than I did about this particular subject.

I had no choice but to play his game.

"And how do I know the right road from any other?" I asked, recalling when I had witnessed that same infinitely curious grid for myself. "What is to say I wouldn't end up in Plato's cave anymore than I would end up in Emily's sitting room?"

"The mushroom knows," Atom said with what appeared on the surface to be supreme confidence. "If you have the right intent, they take you where you need to go."

I wondered for a moment if mushrooms would have any effect whatsoever on my vampyre body, but that was an answer I had possessed since my very first encounter with the mushroom entity.

It, too, was a preternatural being.

You think too much, the beast complained. *Just trust the process.*

After all that had happened that day, trust came even less

easily than it had before.

"When will you leave?" Atom asked, his elfin features more grim than he knew.

My gaze had been fixed on the lightning, my vampyre heart an echo of the approaching thunder.

"When the storm has passed," was all I said.

CHAPTER TEN
The gate of dark desire

I slept.

When I awakened, it was to find myself curled peacefully on one side with Atom pressed up against me, his scarred back to my chest, his rump nuzzling my sleeping phallus. The cadence of his breathing told me he was awake. The irregular rise and fall of his chest said he was weeping.

The direction of the wind was such that a warm breeze was blowing in from the south window, while rain pattered softly from the east and snow had gathered again on the northern sill. Only the west was silent and still, the River of Stars reflecting endlessly into the evernight sky above Smoketree Farm.

The scent of rain and campfire smoke filled the room, combining with the pleasant musk of old books to create a womb that held me in a truly comfortable embrace. Perhaps not surprisingly, a wooden bowl filled with freshly-picked mushrooms sat on the corner of the desk, and I awakened just in time to see the scarecrow leaving through the open door – the closest I had ever come to him.

I should point out that I have never interacted directly with the scarecrow. He is, as near as I can tell, a projection of my will – a faithful servant who is content with his station, but who is also free to leave or evolve or simply vanish altogether should that desire ever overtake him. I neither own him nor command him. He simply *is*, and that has always been a comfort, too.

What happened after that was largely a blur. I rose from the bed with the full intent of ingesting the bowl of psilocybe cubensis mushrooms the scarecrow had left, but instead I became distracted by the images flickering on the laptop. I cannot say precisely how, but between the knowledge I had gleaned from Jason and the large stack of books Atom had conveniently left on the corner of the desk, I found myself thoroughly absorbed in this "internet" experience for what would have been days had time held any meaning.

At the very least, it would allow the blue-stemmed mushrooms to dry and the sentient ally within them to fully awaken.

Because I am not hampered by any traditional human limitations, I read entire volumes in the span of minutes, absorbing and retaining vital information not only about the fascinations the world of the future has to offer, but particularly about the outcomes of elections, races, sporting events and anything and everything upon which a man might place a gentleman's wager.

I studied the movement of key industries, the price of shares, the exact location where Spanish galleons had gone down in rough seas and were later discovered by treasure hunters operating under the name of a company I fully intended to purchase. I made a mental note not to board a ship named *Titanic*, and *never* to get on board something called an airplane should I ever become a musician.

When the time came, I would invest in oil and electricity, pharmaceuticals and technologies, even though it would seem on the surface that other commodities *should* have provided a more profitable yield, but were clearly squelched by those in positions of great power.

All of this knowledge would have been interesting to virtually anyone, but absolutely priceless for one with the ability to move in and out of time itself.

In short, I availed myself of the information required to become a man of means.

When I had absorbed all I could in a single session, I returned to my bed and slid in underneath the large blanket of fur, curling on one side until the length of my body was pressed up against the length of Atom's. Perhaps I should not have indulged my unusual desire for physical comfort, and certainly I should have thought better than to indulge *his*. Still, it seemed harmless enough.

Words the beast had spoken some lost time ago whispered again through my mind. *You should fuck him once in awhile to keep him happy. A happy boy is an obedient boy.*

One thing was certain. Atom was *not* a happy boy. Knowing of my imminent departure from Umberlight had left him brooding and sullen.

While I was at the desk, he had slept most of the time, but had finally awakened. And though he hadn't moved, his quiet snuffling compelled me to ask, "Why are you crying, Atom?"

My voice startled him. "I'm not," he lied.

"Why are you crying?" I asked again.

Neither of us had moved. A single candle in the overhead chandelier sparked to a low burn when I spoke, throwing just enough light to breathe life into the somber shadows.

"I wanted you to like me," he said at last.

"What makes you think I don't?"

He snuffled again and wiped at his eyes with the back of one hand. "I know you want to find Emily again – and I hope you can! I hope you *do*! But..."

I realized then just *how* human Atom still was, how locked in to some notion of fidelity – which I considered a bit ironic considering what I had learned about the culture from which he came in the year 2015.

"You believe that if I find Emily I will never return to you?"

He had turned completely away from me, no doubt to hide his weeping. But because we were spooned together with his head resting on my arm, I felt my wrist become wet with his tears.

"Atom, I made a promise to you that I would at least *try* to give you full immortality," I reminded him, more gentle than I should have been.

"I know, but..."

"But?" I repeated when his voice trailed into a lengthy silence.

"The World Above can be a trap if you're not careful," he

128

warned as if speaking from experience. "Too easy to get caught up in its illusions and forget what's real."

The fact that he was right was little comfort. Even I had lost myself in the strange allures of the World Above more times than I could count. Emily was only the most recent, and now the pull of her was like an unrelenting magnet – not healthy for a mortal, even less so for a vampyre.

But I could not deny it. I had built an entire world in my grief, so how could I turn my back on what might be the only *cure* for that grief?

I decided to be truthful with Atom even though I should have been punishing him for his long list of transgressions, the most recent of which included whining and emotional manipulation, whether intentional or not.

"I do not intend to live with Emily in the World Above, Atom," I explained. "It is my hope to bring her here."

"What about the second ritual?" he asked, sideways to the conversation we were having. "I mean... when did you plan to...? And what do you think she's going to have to say about that? I mean..." He paused, clearly struggling with his emotions. "I mean..."

I had no idea what he meant. "What *do* you mean?"

"I mean... I don't think she's going to be very open-minded about you fucking *me*!" he blurted out at last. "I mean," he said again, and if he repeated those words one more time I swore to myself I might strangle him, "she's from a different *time.* And even if you *do* turn her, she's still going to want that ring on her finger and your dick exclusive to *her*! I mean – that's what women from that time period *expect*, isn't it?"

There was that headache coming on again.

"You worry too much," the beast said, only then waking up. "And about things that do not concern you."

The words were spoken sternly, without apology, without any attempt at tenderness. I was momentarily appalled at myself for my insensitivity when Atom was in such an emotional quandary, and yet...

The first lesson you must learn if you want to be a Creator is the art of brutality.

I simply could not afford to be gentle with him.

Atom sniffled again, went quiet, and then gave an unmistakable sob that seemed to be torn from some forsaken pit at the very bottom of his soul.

At the east window, a bolt of lightning split the sky, but it was already moving to the north. The rain which had fallen hard and steady throughout my distraction at the desk was slowing.

"The storm is passing," I said. The mushrooms had dried and waited only to be ingested. "I will be leaving soon."

Atom sobbed deeply to himself but offered no argument, did not appeal for me to remain, for clearly he knew his pleas would fall on the deaf ears of a man driven by obsession.

"Stop crying now, and kneel for me," I commanded him.

My edict took him off guard, for he sobbed only once more, then turned his head to look at me through swollen eyes set into delicate features carved of sorrow and grief.

"I don't want a mercy fuck, Thorn," he said with a harsh conviction that was impressive under the circumstances.

"Did I ask what you *want*?" I said.

I was already on my knees behind him as my voice deepened and my body hardened. It was remarkably convenient for me to have such a beast within, for it had always been my nature to be tender and considerate with my lovers – traits that would have been to my detriment now. The beast, of course, had no such civilized programming, and would do precisely what needed to be done. It was therefore an easy choice for me to hand control over to him completely.

Somewhere between one thought and the next, my leggings were draped over the foot of the bed, leaving me wearing only the thin, ruffled shirt that was open halfway down my chest, and fell to a point where the hem was just touching the top of my heavily swaying erection.

I thought to remove the shirt, but when I caught sight of

130

myself in the gigantic wooden mirror on the north wall, I liked the portrait it painted and chose to leave it on.

My hair had fallen from its ribbon and draped about my shoulders like a sheltering veil. Atom's expression was reminiscent of some alternate male rendition of The Rape of Proserpina.

The storm crept in to watch on footsteps of rain, little breaths of wind.

"Kneel and lift your robe," I said. "I will not ask you again."

Perhaps I am an old fool, but I had expected him to acquiesce easily – for there was no denying it was *exactly* what he wanted. Instead, curling tightly into a fetal position, he sobbed soul-deep and said only one word.

"*No!*"

While *I* might have taken a moment – even if only one – to ascertain whether his refusal was genuine or only part of a game, the beast within me was thoroughly aroused by *either* possibility, and took it upon himself to throw the blanket aside and forcibly lift the squirming scamp off the bed and then dump him face-down into the thick nest of brocade and velvet pillows.

Atom wailed and sobbed and even began to kick and fight as if for his very life, but it could not be denied that his staff had thickened in response to the mere threat and promise of being mercilessly fucked.

I wished for a moment that I had thought to wish for shackles on each of the four bedposts, but the wish became the quantum manifestation, and in another instant I had captured one flailing arm and secured his wrist into the padded leather cuff, locking it in place with a buckle that would not yield to his fitful protests.

It took little effort to bind the other thrashing limbs, and when the deed was done, he was splayed face down on the bed like some sacrificial offering, his arms stretched out above his head, his legs widely spread, his rump raised up on the little mountain of pillows which were part of my darkling nest. The black robe had ridden up to his waist, and offered no protection to his tender backside or his wounded pride.

He was mine for the taking, and there was an undeniable surge of power which came with that knowledge.

The entire time, he wailed and cursed and yanked hard on the restraints, but I was without mercy for his plight, as I knew I *must* be without mercy. If he could not surrender to me in *this*, he would never be able to surrender to me when his life was suspended in the balance.

For a single moment of horror, I realized that this was all too familiar to me, though from a completely reversed perspective, when I had been the one flailing and wailing, and Ambrose had taken me over his lap to teach me not only that I *must* submit, but to administer the painful consequences that were an automatic byproduct when I *didn't*.

In that moment, I hated myself as Atom must certainly hate me. And yet, just as I had sworn a pact with Ambrose, so had Atom sworn an identical pact with me – an agreement that went beyond words and into the sacred territory of life and death. If he could not learn to surrender, if he struggled and fought during the final ritual when he would be required to literally give up his *life* to me, he would die in the fall and there would be no bringing him back.

You know what you have to do, the beast said, and when I glanced into the mirror again, I saw that a thin wooden paddle had appeared in my hand, undoubtedly summoned into existence at the same time the restraints had manifested. I also saw that Atom's gaze was positively riveted on that mirror as well – and in that way he would be both victim and witness to what was to come.

The beast liked that idea very much.

Resigning myself to the consequences of my own decision and desire to *be* a Creator, I slapped the paddle against my open palm, the cracking sound causing Atom to squirm and clench his eyes tightly shut in what he must have believed was about to be his end.

"You will not look away," I cautioned, lowering the paddle to his trembling rump and rubbing it softly, gently across his skin – a warning of what was to come. "You will watch as each blow falls, and for every time you cry out or beg me to stop, one additional blow will be added. Do you understand?"

He sucked in a harsh breath, eyes wide with a fright which was not in alignment with the straining erection that peeked out from between his wide-spread legs.

"Please... *don't!*" he begged.

"That's one added to the existing five," I said calmly. And with a fair amount of satisfaction, the beast within me brought the paddle down hard and quick against his raised buttocks.

The resulting *crack!* came in precise unison with a loud clap of thunder and a brilliant flash of lightning that threw the room into a momentary brightness which revealed every grim nuance of Atom's plight to the watchful eye of the mirror.

Even though the first blow undoubtedly stung the tender globes, he managed not to cry out, though he *did* bury his face in the pillows and trembled violently.

"Remember what I said," I warned him, raising the paddle for the next blow. "If you look away again, I will add another."

With what seemed to be a real effort, he lifted his head from the pillows and looked again into the mirror, where our eyes met in that bright reflection. Despite the brutality I was unleashing on him, his expression was one of total adoration and undeniable absolution. I didn't need to read his mind to hear his thoughts, which were a tangible presence in the room.

I forgive you, he seemed to be saying. *I forgive you, Thorn.*

But in that moment, I did not want his forgiveness. I had not forgiven Ambrose, and so I did not want to be forgiven. So when the paddle fell for the second time, it was with considerably more force than the first blow – sufficient to cause those intense teal eyes to widen and blink back the tears of pain which blinded him for a moment and fell onto a segment of the bed already wet from his weeping.

To be candid, I was secretly amazed at his endurance. Though he continued to shudder and writhe, and though his buttocks had begun to show a rosy red response to his punishment, he didn't protest the second blow, and even managed to endure the third when I delivered it mercilessly and without warning a few moments later.

But when I raised the paddle in preparation for the fourth blow, he looked at me in the mirror with an expression of such absolute and undeniable *love* that I could barely remain in the same room with him, and had to fight my undeniable instinct to flee.

Just as I did not want him to forgive me, I could not fathom the idea that he really did love me. I *liked* the little demon. Maybe I even loved him the way one loves a dear friend and companion, but I was not *in* love with him the way he was *clearly* in love with me.

Whenever Ambrose had disciplined me as I was now disciplining Atom, I had felt such an abject *loathing* for him that it had blotted out all other feelings. *That* was how I had survived him. *That* was how I had survived even his death kiss which came at the end of the third ritual. And yet, though I did not want to admit it to myself, I could not deny that it was some horrendous and unbidden and completely ghastly moment of *love* for the bastard that had raised me up from the dead.

Perhaps I should not have been surprised to see that I was weeping now, too – not the silver tears of my lifeforce, but the warm and salty tears which were a reminder that I, too, had once been human.

I did not want to be human.

I did not want to *ever* have been human.

I did not want to be loved.

I did not *ever* want to have loved Ambrose, even for a moment.

And so I drew the paddle back and once again struck poor

Atom's tortured backside with such a force that his entire body lurched forward and a raw gasp of torment was torn from his throat. He climaxed against his will, spilling his essence onto a red velvet pillow. His body undulated with uncontrollable spasms, and he cried a single word that was an epitaph to his orgasm.

"*Thorn!*" Then, more softly. "Thorn..."

But because we both knew it wasn't over, I gave him no reprieve, no leniency, no time off for good behavior. Instead, I said the only thing I *could* say under the circumstances, though my voice was hoarse and my tears were falling freely.

"You were told not to cry out," I reminded him, and immediately dealt the fifth blow which landed squarely while his sexual elixir was still flowing. The effect was not what I expected, but what I should have predicted. He became instantly hard again.

"I did not give you permission to climax. Another blow must be added for your disobedience," I told him without sympathy.

In the mirror, I could only gaze with wonder at the resplendent sight we presented. He actually appeared to glow like some holy sacrifice in ecstasy at the thought of its own slaughter. And now, instead of shrinking away from the impending lash of the paddle, he had gotten to his hands and knees and was presenting himself for the final two blows.

He held my gaze. He said my name again, now with a deep reverence. He raised himself higher.

What I could *not* have predicted was that this aroused me perhaps more than anything ever had. My phallus swelled to the point of bursting, and while I wanted nothing more than to slam hard and fast into his uplifted rump and inject him full of my essence, I knew I could not – *dared* not – go back on my dark promise.

Raising the paddle high, I could not hold back a sob that had been building for centuries. A cry of victory – for it was now plain to see that Atom had submitted, surrendering himself to his fate and to my command. I wept openly – a wrenching cry I had never permitted myself to utter when I had been forced to lie across Ambrose's lap and endure a similar discipline that had left me filled with shame and anger, even when I was secretly overwhelmed with gratitude.

I had never dared to explore those memories too closely, for I had never wanted to admit, even to myself, that that moment of total surrender had also been the most profound moment of *power* I had ever known.

You must reward him for his submission, the beast whispered. *Give him what he most desires so that he will give in to you completely when he must.*

When the paddle fell for the sixth time, the sound in the room was like the high-pitched crack of a rifle shot, echoing off the walls and ceiling of the tower and carrying all the way to the four corners of Umberlight.

Tears ran down the imp's face, but he neither cried out nor looked away. When his legs went weak and he collapsed onto the pillows, he hesitated only long enough to breathe, then immediately scrambled back into position and raised himself in preparation for the seventh and final blow.

I was awe-struck by his ability to not only endure the pain, but to actively invite it. My manhood bobbed heavily, an eager companion filled with a demanding need I had seldom experienced. I wanted to rush. I forced myself to go slow instead.

Holding Atom's gaze in the mirror, I lowered the paddle to his tormented rump and once again ran it tenderly over the reddened flesh. He trembled in response. His eyes begged for the deed to be done.

"*Hurry*," he said, just above a whisper. "I need to feel you inside me again."

I very much wanted to hurry, but because he had asked it, I moved slower still. In the mirror, my reflection smiled at him – though it was a dangerous smile straight from the lips of the beast. I lay the paddle on the bed, then ran my bare hands over his backside. The twin globes were hot from their punishment, and quivered in anticipation when I slipped one finger between them to tease at the eager orifice.

"Is this what you want?" I asked, leaning over his back as I pushed into him barely an inch.

He moaned fitfully, lifting himself up, struggling to impale himself even as I held him in check, neither withdrawing nor delving deeper.

"I need it, Thorn," he begged. "*Please!*"

I was without sympathy. "But you've already had your pleasure, spilled it into the pillows before your punishment was complete," I reminded him. "Perhaps I should simply give you your last two blows and then send you to your bed."

At this, I felt him stiffen, tighten. "*Two* blows?" he repeated. "I thought – I mean – I thought there was only *one* more!"

My finger delved a tiny bit further. "Ah... perhaps I lost count," I said as he once again struggled to bring me deeper into him. "Three it is."

As I watched his face in the mirror, he actually paled. When I withdrew my teasing finger and picked up the paddle, quickly returning to my kneeling position behind him for the greatest leverage, he took a deep sobbing breath and simply waited for it to be over.

I did not disappoint him. Because I had *said* there would be three, I had no choice but to deliver on that promise – even though he had done nothing to warrant the additional two. Admittedly, I was enjoying this dark power over him – a power I had never experienced in my very long lifetime.

I delivered the first two blows hard and fast – both of which caused him to groan, both of which brought more tears streaming down his elfinly handsome face. Then, when he made no move to evade me, I brought the paddle crashing down on him for the final time, with such a force that he collapsed face-down on the bed just as I tossed the weapon aside.

I entered him savagely an instant later, driving the entire length of my shaft all the way into him until he grunted with the fullness which must have been twice as brutal as the paddle could ever have been.

In the mirror, his eyes went wide.

The sacrifice had met the blade.

He held my gaze for a moment longer, and an expression of unparalleled contentment caused his eyes to drift shut just as he whispered, "I *want* you to kill me, Thorn."

Time stopped – an interesting phenomenon, since time did not exist here.

At first, I thought I had imagined it – but when he opened those too-bright eyes and our gazes locked in the mirror, I knew there could be no mistake.

If I had had a human heart, it might have stopped or exploded. Instead, I felt a hollow echo in my chest, and before I knew what was happening, absolutely *everything* was out of control.

In that moment, I very much *wanted* to kill him – and yet the dreadful irony was that we had formed an agreement to bring him into an eternal life of full immortality. And though I had not intended for this encounter to be the second ritual in the art of transformation, the beast had bitten mercilessly into his neck before I could even begin to stop it.

It was no secret to me that I did not yet have the power to turn him. And certainly it could be no secret to him either.

What was his agenda? Did he want to *really* die? Was this simply some elaborate suicide by vampyre game he was playing?

I had no answers.

I only knew that his unexpected plea had awakened within me a hunger the likes of which I had not felt since I had first awakened as a vampyre and fed on the warm essence of a mortal. And it was a hunger that did not limit itself to the sudden need for his blood. It was a hunger that drove me to pin him to the bed, prying his legs further apart with my knees, and to then slam into him a second time with a force that would have broken a human in half.

But because Atom was preternatural as well as human, he didn't fracture, though he did scream when I released my bite and descended on him again on the other side, my sharp fangs cutting into him to send the rush of blood jetting into my mouth at the same time I was pounding into his savaged nether regions with my unrelenting staff.

I was out of my mind.

He had finally driven me mad.

And even as that thought came to me, the beast laughed and whispered, *You don't seem to believe me when I tell you he's not what he seems.*

I didn't care *what* he might be.

Something had torn loose inside me when he uttered those words. *I want you to kill me, Thorn.* Had I not warned him that to make such a plea three times would mean his end?

But I was lost, my own dark passion rising to the surface like a wild animal cornered and threatened. It became an entity unto itself – a living, breathing monster whose name was carnal desire held too long in check.

As I drove into him again and again, he began to whimper and moan, weeping in a manner that may have been pain, may have been pleasure.

It mattered not to me either way.

I took him as if I owned him, as if he were clay and I was destined to mold him.

When I could drink no more of him and had drained him to a dangerous point bordering on mutual delirium, I rolled him roughly onto his back, allowing my shaft to slip free at the same time the shackles vanished and we were just two men struggling to keep our heads above the black waters of the true death.

He looked up at me through eyes that were drunk on desire and yet ravaged with pain. But at the same time, he opened his legs to me when I knelt between his knees. When I entered him with our faces only centimeters apart, he rose up to meet my ruthless thrust with an eagerness that was astonishing under the circumstances.

Though I have no memory of how it happened, I found a small knife in my hand, and before I could change my mind, before I could even try to wrestle this madness back under *my* control, I had taken the blade and made an inch-long cut just above the left nipple of my breast.

Grabbing him roughly by the back of the neck, I pulled his mouth to me and compelled him to drink his own blood as it was rushing and coursing through my veins. Somewhere in another world altogether, it occurred to me that even though I had almost emptied his heart entirely, I could not glean even a single thought from his mind, not a whisper of a memory of his past.

He remained a mystery.

And that may have contributed to my uncontrollable desire to *take* from him what rightfully should have been mine.

This was the birth of the demon of dark desire – the second gate required to complete the rituals. This was the cornerbone of carnal need – to do what should never be done, no matter what the cost.

And though I did not fully realize it at the time, this darkest of dark desires was also the balancing force between brutality and love. One must have enough brutality to *do* the unthinkable and enough love to *undo* it when the time came.

And so I took him. I would say I raped him, but as I have already made abundantly clear, Atom was a willing sacrifice and I was merely his sexual executioner.

He lay there beneath me, opening to each thrust and tightening in an effort to hold me inside him with every withdrawal. His own thick phallus was trapped between our bodies, hard as river rock, and slick from the lingering essence of his first release.

I was keenly aware of his mouth attached to the suffering

wound on my breast, and of the wicked tongue that slid deep inside the cut to torment me. As he drank deeper, suckling harder, I could feel the merging of our unique souls which I had not felt since Ambrose had taken me without mercy, and had forced me to drink from him just as I was now forcing Atom.

It was a merging and mingling of pure energy – raw and fierce and as untamed as the heart of a newborn star. It was a coupling not possible between two humans, nor even between a human and a vampyre.

It was the blazing symbiosis of two immortals.

And though Atom was not *yet* immortal, feeling that joining and remembering how it had felt with Ambrose, I began to actively hope – perhaps even *believe* – that I might be able to save him despite himself.

He drank me until I forced his greedy mouth away, and then we were looking at one another, man to man, vampyre to vampyre, as I thrust deep inside him – *once, twice, three times* – and then with a cry of unparalleled satisfaction, I filled him with the raw lava of my immortal essence.

The throbbing of it was so hard and deep that I cried out a second time, throwing my head back and wailing until the walls of the tower trembled and several books flew from the shelves.

Atom endured it all in silence, except for a soft weeping that came as he climaxed between our undulating bodies.

"It burns," he whispered frantically, squirming beneath me and clenching his muscles tight around my fully-embedded weapon. "Like fire... *it burns!*"

It had burned when Ambrose brutalized me in a fashion that was all too similar. It had burned. And it had hurt. And I had craved it more than I would ever confess.

I lay myself down on top of him when it was over, and left our bodies joined in that unforgiving heat.

There were several questions I wanted to demand of the little bastard, not the least of which was why he had done the *one* thing he had been told *not* to do. *I want you to kill me, Thorn.*

The words still echoed in my mind.

But within moments, we were both asleep.

In my dreams, I had him twice more. When I awoke at intermittent intervals, I realized my body was hard again. The dark desire, though briefly satisfied, would not leave me.

I wanted him again. And so I took him while he pretended to sleep.

But no matter how many times I indulged myself utterly with his tortured but willing body, I would awake again drunk on the need to take, but also delirious with the need to give.

My blood.

My animus.

My body.

Eat my body, drink my blood and you will never die, the beast said with a sinister laugh. *Did you think it was all just made up, my little prince?*

I chose *not* to think. Instead, I gave control over to the dark desire, and savagely ravaged the sacrificial lamb until I passed out and slipped into fitful hallucinations where it all just continued to continue.

I had passed the second gate.

~

I woke into the karma of delirium.

Atom was running a hand dipped in melted snow across my brow as I pitched and tossed in what might have been fever dreams had I been even remotely human.

He leaned over me, so close I could count the fairies squatting on his long eyelashes.

"It's all right," he assured me as if he knew. "The first time you turn someone, it changes you, too."

"And how do you know this?" I asked, though my words

were slurred.

He stroked my hair with genuine concern. "I read it in a book."

"What book?"

"This one."

In my condition, that made perfect sense. I didn't bother pointing out that he wasn't turned. Not completely. Not yet. And neither was I.

"Why are you still here?" I wondered, though my words were slurred and might have been spoken in Greek or even High Fae. He could have run away. He *should* have run away.

He ran his hand over my brow again, bent to touch his lips to my forehead.

"Don't you know I love you?" he asked, though it wasn't really a question.

I pulled him to me and kissed him deep and hard instead. I kissed him the way I had kissed Jason, kissed him the way he once said he had *never* been kissed. He came into my arms like a lover then, lay himself down at my side, and rested his head on my shoulder.

"I love you," he said again. "I've loved you since we first met."

"I know," I said, but my voice was barely a whisper and my eyes were threatening to close again. The words he wanted – *needed* – to hear wouldn't come, for they would have been a lie. I loved him but was not in love with him. I had fucked him as I'd never done with any other, but the beast would not allow me to confuse dark desire for the sacred gate of love.

The candle in the overhead chandelier was guttering. The storm had passed. Soon it would be time for me to go.

"For now, it's enough just knowing you know," Atom murmured, curled against my side with one arm thrown possessively over my chest.

More than I ever could have imagined or even hoped for, he had surrendered. He demanded nothing.

And yet...

The raw honesty in those words threatened to set me weeping again. "You need more than that. You *deserve* more than that." It was as open as I'd ever dared to be with him – and it scared me more than a little.

He pressed one finger to my lips to silence me. "It'll come," he said with great confidence and a smile that was warm and genuine and filled with tangible affection. "In time, Thorn. You'll see."

As I lay there in a euphoric stupor, drained of energy and yet paradoxically overflowing with it at the same time, I could only hope he was right.

Brutality.

Dark desire.

Love.

Even though I had passed through the first two gates, the third remained elusive. I *wanted* to love Atom, but perhaps for the wrong reasons. Had my desire to be a Creator become so fierce that I could think of nothing else? Was my obsession with Emily overshadowing a love that was perhaps far more real and had conquered the mysteries of time and space to find me here in the womb of Umberlight?

And what of the humans who had built a cathedral filled with my likeness, and who called me their prince?

Though I had not allowed myself to think of it, there had been odd stirrings in the Firefly Forest, rumors among the fairies of wolves who walked upright and spoke in the voices of men.

The scarecrow had taken to standing at the western-most perimeter of Smoketree Farm, where the pumpkin fields ended and the picket fence stopped, gazing toward the horizon with a cautious demeanor that said something had fallen from the River of Stars. And whereas he had always been a solitary figure, I had occasionally observed a large black bird walking behind him in the fields or perching on his shoulder to whisper secrets only a raven could know into his ear.

In the east, there had been inexplicable glimmerings of light on the Ever-Forking Road – something I had tried to explain away as moonglow reflecting on fog, even while secretly knowing the explanation was nothing so simple.

Something was out there.

Even at that moment, when the world should have been utterly still and empty, a mourning dove could be heard through the north window.

Umberlight was coming to life.

It could no longer be denied. Atom's words came back to me as I lay there in my darkling nest.

"Whether you like it or not, others are coming. And it's going to happen sooner than you think. The fireflies are just the first. You have to know others are coming!"

Maybe I should have rejoiced, for even though I coveted my solitude, there is some truth to the old saying that no man is an island. Nor is any vampyre.

Instead, I realized with an abrupt rush of horror that I was feeling the same crushing sense of grief I had experienced on the day Emily died, the same grief that had driven me from the mortal world and into the self-willed sanctuary of Umberlight.

Perhaps the ultimate and final irony is that the same thing which had brought me here was the same thing which would now cast me out.

CHAPTER ELEVEN
Farewell to Umberlight

When I rose from the bed and stood for a moment in the center of the room, surrounded by this place which had been my sanctuary for so long, I was suddenly overwhelmed by an almost forgotten memory of a time when I had been forced to leave another place that had been a refuge to me...

~

Drunk on the late autumn harvest, Ambrose had summoned me from my chamber – which was more accurately my cell – and I had been brought to him by the two eunuchs who were his personal guards.

In the past, before I had been fully transformed into a vampyre in my own right, such a summoning would normally end with me on my hands and knees and Ambrose ravaging me until I collapsed or until he passed out from too much wine and too much squandered energy. Now, it generally meant some lengthy conversation wherein he did all the talking and I pretended to listen. He called me his confidant, and though there were at least a dozen other vampyres housed on his estate, he seldom if ever summoned any of them to his side.

He wanted me to feel special, or so he said.

I felt apprehensive and angry instead – for even though I was an immortal, I was also still very much his prisoner.

Normally a fiend who found dark humor in almost any situation, he had turned maudlin that night, and while he was sitting underneath an olive tree in his private garden, he had looked up at me with a rare expression of sincerity and maybe even affection.

"Home isn't where you live, you know," he had said.

"No?"

He took another sip of his wine, and looked up at the stars which were so bright they were like wildfires in the sky, jewels on the fingers of the gods.

"For an immortal – or anybody else with any sense – home is the clothes on your back, the shoes on your feet," he murmured, his words only slightly distorted.

It was one of the few times in our long acquaintance I had known him to make a straightforward statement. Something told me he was scared. Even lonely. Looking at him there in the light of the moon which was just rising over the vineyards, I could not deny his physical beauty any more than I could forget the torments I had endured at his hand.

I chose to feel nothing – for in that moment, love and loathing were precisely the same and both were only treacherous indulgences.

"What is it you're trying to say, Ambrose?" I asked, only slightly irritated when he turned somber and spent a long time staring at his feet.

He didn't look up. His voice was barely audible when he spoke. "It's time for you to leave."

He could have said his head was on fire and it would not have surprised me any more. And yet, I had to wonder if he were only toying with me as he often did. Though I had been a vampyre for more than two years now, I had never been permitted to leave the estate. Yes, I was powerful but not yet invincible, but Ambrose was far _more_ powerful and rumor said he was over a thousand years old. The one time I had attempted to escape, the consequences had been dire, and not something I would choose to unleash on the reader just yet.

Ambrose just sat there in his drunken stupor, drawing little symbols in the sand with an index finger. His cinder-black hair fell in thick waves to his neck. His angular features were reminiscent of the dark gods themselves. Many who had endured his torments whispered that he was Hades himself, exiled from Tartarus and hiding in a vampyre's skin.

"Go now," he said with a voice of authority I had come to recognize and, yes, to fear. "Go before I change my mind."

Was it only another ploy? Another game of submission even though I had long ago surrendered to the bastard, even if with a grudge and a hatred I would carry in my heart forever?

Finally he lifted his head and it was then that I saw the tears in

his eyes. Neither human nor animus, they were tears of blood. Red
tears. Tears of grief.

Tears of love.

"Go!" he commanded, and his voice broke. "I will not say it
again!"

I stood there at war with myself for only a moment longer. And
then I ran – though whether from Ambrose or from the avalanche of
contradictory feelings that overcame me, I was never certain. I ran
past the sleeping guards and through the open gate, and I ran until
my maker and my home and my beginnings were far behind me.

When I reached the harbor, I found an old merchant ship bound
for Italy and stowed away in her belly, where I remained for weeks.

Only in hindsight did I realize he had loved me enough to
finally let me go.

I never saw Ambrose again.

~

Was I only running again?

The night which had embraced Smoketree Farm was
sentient, but no longer entirely silent. The crickets who had
sung only in the City of Tempest had found their way through
the fog and come to dwell in the fields. A wayward firefly
fairy had alighted on the southern sill and sat looking in the
window at me, her tiny wings unmoving, her brilliant violet
eyes seeming to hold some great secret known only to the fae.

Atom had fallen into a deep and restful sleep in the
middle of my bed, and though there were volumes I should
have said to him – not knowing what in all the worlds *to* say –
I chose instead to leave a letter on the glowing rectangular eye
of the laptop.

Atom... my friend, my companion...

Since you already know I am leaving for a time, I hope it
will come as no surprise when you find me gone. You were

sleeping — so much like an innocent child you seemed — and I did not want to wake you.

It is my hope that you will look over Umberlight in my absence, and consider it your home for as long as you choose to remain. There have been — as I'm sure you have observed — peculiar stirrings throughout the land. As you predicted, others will be coming. Undoubtedly, some are already here.

I will say once again that it is my hope and my intent to give you your heart's desire — the final kiss of the ritual which will make you truly immortal and create a bond between us that will outlast Time itself.

What I know at this moment is that love is the answer — the third and final gate through which I must pass in order to become what I must — but I also must be cruelly honest when I say that I do not yet possess that answer.

In dreams and visions, I have come to see that my heart must learn to open again. It must learn to sing as well as weep. It must learn to love as well as it has learned to be brutal and desirous.

Until then, I am only a lonely vampyre.

I am going to the World Above to find my heart again, you see. I hope to awaken it in Emily's embrace, as I once did, but I have also come to realize the truth in a particular bit of wisdom found on the internet: No one can step in the same river twice.

Nothing is ever as it once was. The water is always flowing, the river is always changing. That is simply the way of the world — not just the world above, but all the worlds, including Umberlight herself.

That which does not change cannot grow.

These are only words of course, struggling to communicate what words have never been able to capture. Time. Sex. Death. Love. The four cardinal integers in the grand equation.

Know this, my dear friend: when I find my heart and my love, I will bring them back here and give them to you in a kiss that will make you free forever.

Until then...
Dream of me in the night,
Thorn

When I looked up from the monitor, the mushrooms were gone and I was beginning to feel very much at one with the spirits of the air and with Grandmother Spider, who sat at the very heart of the multiverse, spinning the grid of Time into being.

The sentient mushroom ally whispered that I must hurry to the first crossroads I would find along the Ever-Forking Road, turn left at the intersection of Twisted Infinity and Infinite Possibility, and follow the rainbow cast by the light of Yesterday's moon.

Then I was flying.

CHAPTER TWELVE
The World Above

Once I lost my mind beneath a wooden bridge
* where mushrooms grew wild and speckled,*
* delectable eggs of the fertile cosmic womb.*
Vampyres are gluttons
* so I played there crazy to the bone*
* watching the moonfall*
* and the rainshine night*
* drinking the stars in my cupped hands.*

The sky was on fire.
The river was aflame.
After the moon had set, the demon-fruit bloomed and
some madman said, "Let there be light."

I scooped up the sun, evil morning flower,
* to steal its reflection from the river*
* dribbling it through my fingers*
* until it was gone.*
It came back of course,
* fractured water all aglow, mending.*
So I beat at it with a willow stick
* until it turned wrong side out*
* and sank to the bottom,*
* a popped yellow balloon.*
Scholars said it was only an eclipse.
* I know better.*
I won the soul of the sun that once,
* because I was crazy enough*
* to believe I could.*

I must have lain on the riverbank for hours that day. The
mushroom and I had spoken at length about the nature of
time, the dark side of sex, the ubiquitous non-entity of death,

and the catalytic force of love. For the most part, we were in agreement, except we had argued vehemently about the quantum structure and even the questionable existence of this thing known as death.

While I maintained that death was a cessation of life and in all probability a complete termination of awareness, the mushroom had argued that *he-and-she* (for it was both) were but petals of a much larger organism, and that even if the petals should fall, the organism itself would remain and the mycelium from which he had fruited was a vast and flourishing system which would send up new fruits and petals endlessly.

"I cannot die for I am always alive," he maintained. "I cannot die for death is only another illusion."

I strongly disagreed, imploring Petal (as he had named himself) to gift me with the wisdom and the power to *be* a Creator so that the petals I most loved would never have to fall.

The mushroom proclaimed his immortality through continuity of community, while I argued to the point of distraction for a unique and absolute singularity of consciousness which I had come to call, simply, *I-Am.*

It is impossible to win an argument with a mushroom. It is absurd to even try. They are patient, stubborn creatures who think they know everything.

Generally speaking, they probably do.

But as for the specific understanding of death, I could not agree with the talkative fungi, and so we left our conversation at an impasse and with the agreement to continue it at some other timeless time.

By the time the night had ended, this little Petal had led me through the portals and passageways of the quantum void, and had brought me at last to this riverbank in what he assured me was "the right and proper landing."

And so, it was on that riverbank in the early hours of an autumn morning that I fought my battle with the sun and eventually beat it into submission. But just as I was preparing to celebrate, I heard the sound of approaching footsteps, and looked up through my psilocybin haze to see a young man carrying a metal water bucket approaching my sanctuary beneath a small wooden footbridge.

Only then did I begin to regain some minimal semblance of rationality, some structure of self, which the mushroom had disintegrated almost entirely. I had no recollection of how I had come to be underneath the bridge with a large stick in my hand, nor could I even vaguely imagine *where* I might be.

For a moment, I was concerned that the man might try to harm me, for I had temporarily forgotten that I am a being of light. While in my humanesque manifestation, I was lean and had been referred to as cat-like, and the blacksmith – for he could be nothing else judging by his leather apron and the tools tucked into his belt – was far more muscular and carried himself with a confidence that said he had never been defeated in a fight.

"I'm sorry," I said, though he was still too far away to hear my delirious mumblings. "Is this your bridge? I hope I didn't damage your sun." I assumed it was still lying on the bottom of the shallow stream, but when I leaned over to look, I lost my balance and tumbled with all the grace of a wounded yak into the frigid water.

Surely the man *would* kill me now, for I had almost certainly landed on that elusive sun and maybe even scared it away for good. I splashed and flailed, struggling to stand, but the air was slippery and something seemed to be terribly wrong with my head.

The next thing I knew, the man had grabbed me by one arm and was pulling me out of the river, where I had been attempting to stand. Not on my feet, but on my head.

"And a good morrow indeed!" the stranger said with a laugh as he quite literally spun me right-side up and stood me on my feet. "What a night *you* must have had!" He held onto my arm to steady me, and his hand was warm and strong and undeniably human. "You all right there?"

I blinked, temporarily blinded by river silt and the water still pouring off my hair. Though he spoke flawless English, his accent carried a slightly French intonation. In reality, we began to converse in the language and speech patterns of the day, but since so much of that might be considered archaic and incomprehensible, I shall present the conversations in plain and simple words, omitting any future 'good morrows' or 'good sirs' or 'my lord' and 'my lady' and any other such extraneous chatter.

"Who am I-Am?" I asked. Even I could hear the slur in my words. I tried again. "Where I-Am?" Not much better.

The blacksmith gave a warm laugh that reminded me of someone I had known many, many years ago. Someone now long gone, a fallen petal.

"I can't say who *you* are, but my name is Dariell Royce, and people around here call me Dare."

As he spoke, he was leading me up the steep embankment until we came to a natural knoll where he urged me to sit down. Having rescued me from my embarrassing plight, he could have just left me there to dry, but instead he sat down at my side and kept one hand on my shoulder to prevent me from pitching forward.

It occurred to me that he was looking at me the way one might study some rare species of bird previously believed extinct, but because I was still delirious, I couldn't be sure.

I blinked again, and when I could see a bit better, I could only gaze at this man with true and pure wonder.

Dare was perhaps the most magnificent human male I had ever seen, and though my assessment might be partially attributed to my lingering disorientation, my observation was nonetheless accurate and I would not have stood for anyone trying to refute it.

He was an inch or two shorter than myself, but still much taller and far more athletic in build than most men of the time period – assuming, of course, I was in the late 17th Century at

154

all. His hair was some fantastical shade of moonglow. Perfectly straight, thick and silken, it hung nearly to his waist, yet it was of a color that could not be named at all. To say he was blond was to say a white tiger was just another tabby cat. To say it was golden was to make him common. And this man was anything but common.

As for his face...

I would have said he must be a sculptor's masterpiece escaped from the marble were it not for his attire which clearly marked him as a working man. His features were warmly tanned from the sun and strangely angelic, yet far from the kind of innocence one might expect from any holy angel. There was a strength to his jaw, a beauty that was neither feminine nor masculine to his brow, and an intensity to his golden-brown eyes that was reminiscent of a leopard's hypnotic gaze.

What I liked about him – among everything else – was that he didn't flinch or glance away when he knew I was looking at him. He just smiled openly and gave me the same kind of acute visual examination I had been giving to him.

Some amount of time passed. The sun had crawled out of the river and ascended its secret ladder until it was close to midpoint in a sky of cornflower blue.

Dare didn't try to engage me in absurd small-talk, didn't need to fill the stillness with echoes of his own prattle. We sat together in comfortable silence – something most humans cannot do even after years of friendship. When he did speak, his words took him straight to the point.

"We need to get you up to my place and out of those wet clothes before you catch your death of pneumonia," he said, standing up and offering a hand to assist me.

While I didn't tell him that I wasn't likely to die of pneumonia or any other human sickness, I did like the idea of getting out of my wet clothes. I would have liked it a great deal more if he had volunteered to join me, but I blamed *that* wicked thought on the dark conspiracy between my beast and the surprisingly sensual Petal.

I also liked the prospect of accepting the hand Dare was holding out to me, and though I was now more or less mentally and physically stable again – or so I thought – I took his outstretched palm, once again admiring his strength as he pulled me easily to my feet.

For a few seconds longer than necessary, he continued holding onto me, and once again I saw some glimmer of *something* go darting through his eyes. Recognition? Invitation? Panic?

Or maybe it was just a trick of the brutal light.

Though I was not in any real danger from the sun, it did have the effect of making me disoriented, largely because I had not been exposed to it for such long periods of time since before I had breathed the evernight of Umberlight into being. Other than the brief hours spent in the Parish of Mortality with Atom, I had not seen the sun – and certainly had not missed it – in what might have been decades or more if time had had any meaning there.

We were walking side by side, and though I did not immediately understand it, I began to feel intensely drawn to Dare, as if I had known him before or was somehow destined to know him forever.

It was not a thought I wanted to entertain just then, for the woes of Umberlight and my unfinished task with Atom still weighed heavily on my mind. And so I made a genuine effort to behave as a gentleman, to play the role of the inebriated fool who had wandered too far from town and lost his way at the bottom of the blacksmith's creek.

But even as that thought settled around me, something Atom had said came tumbling across the path and stopped me as surely as if I'd run headlong into a wall.

'The mushroom knows. If you have the right intent, they take you where you need to go.'

I stood in the middle of the narrow dirt path that led up from the riverbank and into a thicket of hawthorn and ash trees a short distance ahead – the edge of a forest that looked menacing and suddenly very dark.

So there I was, a vampyre drenched in the noonday sun and irrationally afraid of the darkness that lay ahead. I could not decide which was worse – the trepidation itself or the annoying symbolism contained within it.

...they take you where you need to go...

It was the word *'need'* to which I should have paid much greater attention before ingesting that know-it-all mushroom.

What one *needs* and what one *wants* are seldom the same.

Dare was a few steps ahead by the time he realized I had stopped. Turning, he shot me a smile. "Don't worry – I don't bite," he assured me.

I didn't tell him that *I* might. His words took me off guard, for I didn't believe they were just a coincidental turn of phrase. Something about his manner said he knew more than he was willing to reveal. He did not have the demeanor of a man assisting a stranger. Instead, Dare seemed to know me.

Listen to your instincts, the beast cautioned, at last emerging from whatever mushroom-induced wet dream had swallowed him for a time. He yawned, stretched, slowly coming to full awareness. Then, looking through my eyes at Dariell Royce, the fiend stood up inside my vampyre skin and perused the blacksmith the way a rogue wolf might peruse a prize lamb. *Oh my goodness badness!,* he commented. *Look what's for dessert!*

I slapped the dastardly brute down so hard that there was an earthquake on the other side of the world.

All of this happened in the span of a single moment, and while the beast was still reeling, I regained control of myself and went back to playing the role I had chosen.

"Please accept my apology for my lack of manners in failing to introduce myself" I began, attempting to smile in a manner that would not reveal my fangs. "My name is Thorn." Normally I have no need of a last name, but I quickly made one up. "Thorn Ambrose."

I was more addled than I realized. It vexed me no end that I automatically took my Creator's name – but once the words were past my lips, there was no pulling them back.

Dare returned my smile, unaware of the multiple conflicts taking place inside my head. "No apology necessary, Thorn. You were pretty much out of this world when I found you down by the creek. And besides, I'm not much for social formalities anyway."

I was liking him more and more.

"Nor am I," I agreed. Little did he know just how true those words were.

Taking a moment to study my surroundings, I began to stabilize inside the confines of the existing time and place. Wildflowers blooming along the creek bank dusted the air with a scent of heather and bluebells. Because of my enhanced hearing, I could detect the clatter of an occasional carriage on a larger road some distance away.

Nothing was familiar.

"I must have wandered farther than I realized from the pub," I said, "Where – exactly – are we?" I paused, then decided to go for broke. "And if I may be so bold, what day is this?"

Now the blacksmith laughed again, which immediately put me at ease despite the paranoid squirming of the beast, who was bound and gagged somewhere in the vicinity of my solar plexus. And though Dare looked at me as if I'd gone daft, he indulged my madness enough to answer my peculiar questions.

Walking the few steps back to where I remained halted, he stood only a foot away, so close I could detect the hot, clean scent of his body. So close I could hear the beat of his mortal heart.

I wanted him.

To say anything else would have been a lie. I had grown accustomed to having my way with Atom whenever I felt the stirring, and though I might have *wanted* to be a gentleman, I had come to like my dark desire and even my brutality.

You sucker-punched me halfway to Bangkok for saying a lot less, the beast complained.

But I had no time to indulge him when Dare started to speak.

"As to the first question, we're a few kilometers outside of London," he said with a little chuckle of amusement. "And as for the second question, it's November 22nd."

I felt a very small measure of relief. At least I was in the right *place.*

I met Dare's curious gaze and tried to feign an attempt at humor. "And the year?"

Lame, the beast pronounced, struggling to gnaw through his restraints even though his comments went ignored.

To my surprise, Dare slapped me on the shoulder in a gesture of male camaraderie, then slipped an arm around my back and began leading me once again down the path as if it were the most natural thing in all the worlds.

"I want some of what *you* were drinking!" he decided with another easy laugh. "But for what it's worth, it's 1664." Noticing my curiosity about our surroundings, he added, "Normally there would be a lot more people on the road this time of day, but that eclipse this morning sent them scurrying for their churches and their prayer books or whatever silly talisman they hang onto whenever the sun and the moon do their little dance every once in awhile."

Perhaps it should not have surprised me to discover that Dare was obviously an educated man.

"So you are not religious?" I surmised.

He tossed his head back and laughed with great amusement. "Not just no, but *hell* no!" he assured me. "My wife and daughter still buy into all that mumble-jumble, but I can't see my way clear to worship a god who would create this beautiful world and these beautiful people, and then just let it all go to hell."

Something inside me fell and soared at the same

paradoxical time. His dislike of absurd religions clearly matched my own and yet...

"You have a family." My statement may well have sounded like the last words of a doomed man.

Dare had removed his arm from my shoulder, and stopped along the path for a moment to pull his hair back and tie it with a leather string. For a reason I could not immediately pinpoint, it seemed he might be attempting to evade my inquiry, even though he himself had brought up the subject.

"Danielle – my daughter – just turned ten last August," he said at last, with a matter-of-fact tone. "She does well in school, says she wants to be a doctor when she grows up."

"A noble ambition," I commented, though my vampyre heart was dangerously silent. "And your wife?"

Again that hesitation, perhaps perceptible only to a being such as myself with acutely heightened senses. "She's a teacher at Danielle's school," he said, though now he was walking again and I had to hurry to catch up. "I tell ya – I'd just as soon head out for the New World, but neither of them want to leave England."

"The New World," I mused, hoping to draw him out and frankly grateful to change the subject. "Why so?"

"The future is coming – faster than any of us can imagine. Soon enough, London will be a thriving city full of wonders you and I can't even begin to imagine," he predicted. "At least in the New World, there'll be a lot more horses needing shoes than here in London." He paused, then added darkly, "A man needs to work. At least that's what we're taught, yes?"

I nodded thoughtfully. "Indeed. It is what we are taught." But it was the death of humans. Not the work but the belief that it was the only road open to them – soldiers in service to the common good, one foot in front of the other, from the cradle straight to the grave.

That subject was far too immense to open just then.

I could not help but wonder if Dare had precognitive

abilities, for the kind of progress he had forecast was indeed coming. I had seen it on the stolen laptop in the tower. And I had felt it in my preternatural bones.

In that way, Dare's dilemma wasn't dissimilar to my own. The world as he had known it was coming to an end, and while it wouldn't be within the span of his human lifetime, it *was* coming, just as unavoidable change had found its way even into Umberlight.

It began to slowly dawn on me that I had not met this man by accident. At some level I had come to understand as quantum entanglement, our destinies were linked.

...they take you where you need to go...

More than simply wanting him as a man might want another man, or as a vampyre might want a human, I wanted to *know* him. Intuitively and without any explanation whatsoever, I wanted this man to be my friend.

The beast would have rolled his eyes if I'd let him. Instead, he just kept chewing at the bindings and shot me a dirty, longsuffering look which said: *Are you going to get all philosophical and mushy every time you're hungry?*

I ignored him completely, far more interested in Dare. "When will you go? To the New World, I mean?"

Dare made a little sound that might have been derision. "I'm sure I *won't*," he said.

"Oh? If it is your desire, why would you not act on it?" Admittedly, I was pushing him.

We walked in silence for several minutes, gradually moving away from the river and into the thickening forest of trees.

"It's not just about me, you know," he replied easily.

Why I was pushing him, I could not have said. It simply began to happen. "You put the happiness and well-being of others above yourself, even if it means giving up something you very much want or even *need* to do?"

The effect of moving from sunlight into shadow was profound – the filtering of light through leaves fluttering in the light breeze. The extreme sense of relief I experienced when the canopy of green closed over us like a comforting veil.

Dare considered my most recent comment in silence for nearly a full minute. Finally he said, "Isn't that what love is all about? Sacrificing your own needs for someone else's?"

A wren high in the trees above us trilled into a soft song. The breeze turned warm, then went still as if stopping to listen.

I considered my response carefully, for even though I knew nothing about this stranger, I had known him all my life.

It's just low blood sugar, the beast insisted. *You need a drink.*

I slapped another gag on him, though he was becoming more difficult to control. I *did* need a drink... and maybe a lot more than that.

"It seems to me that love should also be about compromise," I offered reasonably. "If you are willing to sacrifice *your* needs for others, should they not be willing to sacrifice theirs for you?"

This gave the blacksmith a moment of pause. He slowed his pace, walking now with his hands behind his back and his head lowered in obvious contemplation.

The wind was running her fingers through his hair, tossing loose strands of molten platinum around his sun-and-shadow-dappled face until I thought I might faint at the absolute perfection of his masculine beauty.

You are one smitten kitten, the fiend mumbled around his gag, sounding very much like Atom in that moment.

"I wish I had the answer to that, but I honestly don't," Dare confessed. "Anytime more than one person is involved, not everybody gets what they want."

But I could see the conflict I had awakened in him, and what surprised me was that I had done it with deliberate intent and surgical precision.

Ambrose had torn my world apart with questions alone,

162

undermining all of those deeply-held belief systems I had once accepted as truth when, in reality, they were only intangible ideas put onto me for the convenience of others. Was it now my intention to do the same with this gentle soul who was not nearly as gentle as he wanted me to believe?

I felt sorry for him, for no other reason than that he had had the misfortune to cross my path.

"I'm sorry, my friend," I said, though even that was another subtle program being put onto him. Calling him 'my friend' suggested that we *were* friends. "It's not my place to question, is it? After all, we've only just met."

Though he appeared to breathe a little easier, the deepening of his aura told me I had accomplished precisely what I had set out to accomplish. I had made him question *himself*.

He didn't try to come up with some clever response as a lot of men might have done. Just a smile – though perhaps a shade darker than it had been before.

"It's not much further," he said as if concerned for my well-being. "Just around the next bend."

There it was again. That sense of foreboding I could not fully identify.

"I would not want to intrude on your family," I said, slowing my pace and feeling some inexplicable danger that had nothing to do with my immortal body and everything to do with my immortal soul. (Yes, vampyres have an immortal soul, all myths to the contrary notwithstanding.)

"Not to worry," he said easily. "We're going to my shop. The house is in the city. I don't go up there except on week's end. The good life may be there, but the good work is out here on the road."

I wondered why I read a lot more into his words than he might have intended. Perhaps I only *wanted* to believe he was a solitary animal like myself despite the fact that he had a wife and child. Perhaps I only *wanted* to think he was manufacturing excuses for hiding out in his shop rather than going through the traditional motions of home, family and God.

When we came around that final bend in the path and the trees gave way to sunlight, my fears diminished considerably. No demons or dragons were waiting at the crossroads where the path emptied onto a much wider cobblestone thoroughfare which must have been a corridor between London and Greenwich.

Perhaps a hundred meters or so off the road was what I recognized as a blacksmith's shop. A fire burned in the open forge. Two handsome horses grazed in a pasture behind the work area, and a small dwelling was nestled back among the willow trees.

"Home sweet shack," Dare said with a grin and a gesture of welcome. "It's a far cry from the queen's mansion, but it beats going back and forth every day, and there's more than enough business out here on these cobblestone roads."

At my look of confusion, he added, "The cobblestones are hell on horseshoes. But no matter – let's get you cleaned up and dried out."

By this time, the beast had succeeded in chewing through his restraints. And as I followed Dare to the door of the small cottage, the fiend reared his nasty head to say, *Sure you want to know what's behind the green door? Whips and chains, perhaps? Who gets tied up? You or me? How about him?*

"Shut up," I muttered, not realizing I'd spoken aloud.

Dare had gone a few steps ahead of me and didn't hear my grumblings. Opening the door – which had not been locked – he gestured me inside with a warm and welcoming smile.

As I entered from the brightness of day into the comforting darkness of shadows, I noticed only that dwelling was more or less a large single room set up for efficiency. A narrow bed against the western wall. Wood-burning stove in the tiny kitchen, still glowing from the morning's fire. A few cupboards, most of which had no doors. A humble wooden desk. A foot locker containing clothing. A small pile of tattered books. In the northeast corner, a sheet had been hung from the ceiling, presumably a privacy shield to conceal a water closet.

Dare moved immediately to the foot locker and began rummaging through the tousled garments until he came up with a clean shirt similar to the one I was wearing, and a pair of green velvet leggings which seemed incongruous for a blacksmith's station.

"I think these'll fit you," he said, tossing the clothes onto the bed. Seeing my curiosity about the leggings, he chuckled. "My wife bought them for me when we were newly wed." His expression darkened, and there it was again – something he wasn't saying. "I only wore them once."

It could not be denied that he was nervous, although about what, I could not have said.

I picked up the thin shirt and began going through the motions of unfastening the lashings on the sleeves of my own wet garment. I obviously couldn't tell Dare that I could have changed clothes with a thought long ago. I couldn't tell him I had allowed him to bring me here because it was *my* dark desire to be precisely where I was.

"Oh – I'll wait outside," he offered, and moved toward a narrow door at the back of the cottage.

Oh, how perfect! the beast commented gleefully. *He's shy! Or he thinks you are. Either way, this is going to be fun!*

"No need to put yourself out in the cold," I said, though I could not deny that the fiend had slipped his chains. But because I would not permit him to *be* the fiend he was, we came to a shaky agreement that I would remain in control and have the final say where Dare was concerned.

Having unfastened the sleeves, I pulled the damp shirt over my head before the blacksmith had a chance to retreat.

Seduction is an artform.

It is not a matter of stripping naked and pouncing upon one's prey with all the finesse of a horny schoolboy. It is instead a matter of slow reveals and unspoken promises.

I stood there next to the bed for a moment, pretending to fold my wet shirt before laying it on the floor, and the whole time I was keenly aware of Dare's eyes on me. I could feel his gaze as surely as if it were the wind, and there was no denying that he was appreciative and more than a little curious.

In the past, my lovers had flattered me for my body. My chest was smooth and devoid of hair, my abdomen lightly rippled with the alluring musculature of an athlete. In reality, of course, I could have appeared as a toothless beggar or a boyish urchin, but somewhere along the way I had settled into the vessel I had always envisioned, and the vessel humans seemed to find most appealing.

Having discarded my own shirt, I picked up the one Dare had given me, and began pulling it over my head. I had halfway expected him to step forward to help – the beast had actively prayed to the dark gods for that to happen – but he just stood there watching as if truly mesmerized.

Fortunately, the shirt was long enough to conceal the fact that I was becoming aroused, so when I wriggled out of the leggings and dropped them on top of the discarded shirt, the most mysterious aspects of my vampyre body remained artfully hidden beneath the long hem of the blacksmith's shirt.

Moving slowly, but also with deliberate intent, I stepped into the green velvet leggings and began drawing them up my calves, past my thighs, and eventually arranging them in position at my waist.

When the all-too-human chore of getting dressed had been completed, I looked up and met the stranger's gaze with a smile that allowed him to see just the tips of my fangs.

"Much better," I said. "Thank you."

He continued looking at me with an expression that was ripe with both admiration and a very healthy dose of fear.

"Is everything all right?" I asked, entirely innocent.

Time hung suspended between us. I do believe I saw him

go pale. Though I knew precisely what I was doing, I had no idea *why* I was doing it. We *had* just met, as I have already mentioned. And while he was physically extraordinary and admittedly desirable to me, I was not in the habit of blatantly seducing strangers – particularly those who claimed to be in love with their wife and committed to their family.

Unlike the beast, I was not a complete fiend.

"You came," the blacksmith said, though his voice was barely a whisper. "I was starting to think I'd imagined you."

His words took me off guard. "I'm sorry. I don't understand." I really didn't.

For nearly a full minute, he didn't move, didn't even seem to be breathing. Our gazes remained locked, neither of us looking away. In the dim light of the cottage, he might have been a statue and I might have been his shadow.

But then, coming to some unspoken decision, he drew back the hanging sheet to reveal the secret he had been hiding.

In the corner of the room was an altar. Not a religious altar, nor even a sacrilegious one. Not even a pagan altar in the strictest sense.

Undoubtedly carved of solid mahogany by Dare's own hands, it might have passed for a low bookshelf were it not for the herbs and artifacts strewn across its surface and at its base. Artemisia absinthium – from which absinthe could be distilled, and which was also known by the name 'wormwood.' Amanita muscaria – a distant cousin of the same type of mushrooms which had brought me here. Agrimony – used by sorcerers to summon the spirits of the air. African dream root – a potent herb well known for its ability to induce potent dreams and travels outside the body.

In addition to the many herbs, a goblet filled with polished bloodstones sat on the altar's north corner. On the southern corner was a hand-forged blade bearing symbols from the Egyptian Book of the Dead – and there was no mistaking the stains on the knife, nor the dark red drops which had been left as an offering in a cup of wine.

Not the blood of animals, but the blood of a man. The blood of the man standing in front of me.

All of these things had one thing in common: they were tools for summoning the immortals.

I knew this because I was no stranger to magic, and before I was a vampyre, I had summoned my maker in a similar fashion, as I have already revealed.

Whatever else Dare might have been, he was also a powerful witch – for I could not deny that my uncanny and relentless attraction to him was far more mystical than rational.

I had seen him in dreams.

I had known him in a hundred or more lives somewhere out there along the Ever-Forking Road, where every infinite possibility existed and was made manifest, whether we were ever aware of it consciously or not.

I *knew* him.

And yet I did not know him at all.

"Who *are* you?" I asked, but even as I spoke, the words came simultaneously from *his* mouth.

Neither of us moved, for some inexplicable spell had brought us together and was binding us with an intensity that had caused the sun to flee from the sky, the wind to stop in a reverent pause, and the world to go utterly still.

I was remembering how I had felt when I first summoned Ambrose into my dreams – yet in the end they had turned out not to be dreams at all, but out of body experiences which were not out of body at all.

Nothing unreal exists.

I had been only a man at that time, frightened and filled with deadly wonder, yet not *daring* to believe that my beliefs had taken root in the universe and stepped into the world of matter and men in the form of an immortal.

I was human then.

I was mortal.

Defenseless.

168

Now, my life was coming full circle. Dare was the man filled with questions and fears and vulnerabilities and I was the answer to his darkest prayers, his dangerous magic.

The sense of obligation which came with that knowledge was enormous and yet I would not have traded it for all the wealth in the world. I would not have traded it even for Emily.

Eventually, I saw Dare start breathing again, and to his credit, he never broke eye contact. Any sane man would have bolted, gone running all the way back to London where the streets were brightly lit and all the well-to-do men and women had silently and vehemently agreed there was no such thing as vampyres.

Dare had no such common sense, and that was just one more reason I began falling deeper – and with great willingness – under his spell, just as he had already fallen hopelessly under mine.

He took a step toward me in that tiny room, until we were only inches apart and I could feel the warm breath of him on my cheek. Then, reaching out to me, he placed one hand flat on my chest, where my vampyre heart had begun to beat like a slow and powerful drum. The other hand went to the back of my head, his fingers tangling in my hair.

He pulled my head down to rest on his shoulder, folding me into a commanding embrace until my lips were pressed to the wildly fluttering artery in his neck.

I was powerless to stop myself.

I pierced him slowly. Deeply. And though his entire body shuddered in my arms, he never cried out and never tried to break away as so many mortals did when it finally came to *this*. Instead, he gave himself to me freely, without hesitation and without resistance.

He had placed his fate in my hands and was at peace with whatever the outcome might turn out to be.

When the essence of him burst onto my tongue with the force of an exploding sun, I was the one who gave a little gasp and bore him to his knees as we dropped together onto the bare wooden floor. He was the father of the lightning and the flash point of the storm. October's son. Winter's consort. So many memories swimming in the tumultuous sea of his *Life*.

I wanted nothing more than to devour him utterly, to draw out every nuance of him and take it into myself where I might hold onto it forever. But with the last shred of sanity I possessed, I released my hold on him and lifted my head just enough to meet his eyes.

Though he was weak from allowing me to drink so deeply from him, he managed a little smile that could not have been captured in a thousand words.

Then, leaning forward, he kissed me with the tenderness of a virgin on my lips which were still wet with his life's blood.

""Tell me it's real," he said, his voice thick with emotion. "And if it isn't, let me die before I wake."

Standing at the very threshold of the third gate – which suddenly contained all the terror of the abyss itself – I held him close and rocked him in my arms until we were both fast asleep.

EPILOG
It's complicated

A sliver of a silver moon had crept up out of the void and was peeking in the window over the blacksmith's cluttered desk. Sometime earlier, I had lifted Dare onto his narrow bed and fell in at his side, and now I lay there trembling, listening to the distant song of the creek as it gurgled along through the night like some lost and lonely ghost train seeking a destination that no longer existed.

The mushroom had long since left me, and yet I continued to feel disoriented, dizzy, and filled with an emotion I could only define as abject terror.

Dariell Royce had bewitched me.

Not with his magical practice, not with his incantations or the spilling of his own blood into the Cup of Eternity.

He had bewitched me simply by existing. He had bewitched me with his smile and his laughter and with a single kiss that had been an invitation which I should have politely declined.

Told you so, the beast said. While I was lying there contemplating slipping away into the forest and pretending that kiss never happened, the fiend was considering whether to begin the blacksmith's lessons with the art of brutality or the unleashing of my darkest of dark desires.

This one is different, I said, as much to remind myself as to warn the beast back into his lair. *He is not like Atom. I will not brutalize him into submission. If he is to become immortal at all, he will come to me willingly.*

Did you go to Ambrose willingly? the fiend asked, pretending an interest even though he already knew the answer.

Curled against my back in the tiny bed, Dare stirred just a little, pressing closer for warmth in his sleep. Despite the glowing orange embers of a fire dying in the wood burning stove, the air in the room was cold. Wind crept under the door and through the gaps in the floorboards.

This wasn't a cozy little cabin in the woods for the convenience of a working man. It was a warlock's humble sanctuary – and that, too, was part of the summoning. Just as I had given up my home and my past and even my soul for the prospect of summoning Ambrose, so had Dare left it all behind to demonstrate his commitment and offer his obedience to me.

This realization did not fill me with power, as the beast might have preferred.

It humbled me.

This man was offering me his soul, and it was an offering so pure that I came perilously close to weeping.

For a time, I found myself longing for Umberlight, for my bed in the tower which was large enough to hold four men, where the room was always pleasantly warm unless I wanted it to be otherwise, where the night never ended and the sun never rose over Smoketree Farm.

I wanted this man to be comfortable. I wanted to pamper him and spoil him and dress him in silk and lace just so that I might undress him with reverence and respect and all the affection he deserved.

Smitten, the beast said again. *If it's not low blood sugar, it's gotta be love.*

The fact that the demon dared to utter the word almost made me bolt from the very thought of it.

I could be brutal. I could surrender to my dark desires.

But did I have the courage to *love*? What being in their right mind would *ever* consent to such a thing?

Goes with the job description, the fiend reminded me with no sense of gentleness at all. *You want to be a Creator, you have to open that broken heart of yours to Cupid's arrow – even if you know damn well it's gonna hurt.*

The hurt was too great. When I had lost my wife and son, the wound was so deep it had driven me mad – mad enough to hand my freedom and my body over to a vampyre who had ravaged and savaged me for years. When I lost Emily, the grief was so unbearable it had sent me into a centuries-long coma from which Umberlight had risen as a sanctuary where I could *hide* from Death.

Are you hiding from Death or running from love? the fiend asked with casual disinterest, the same way I might have tried to manipulate a human.

But once the question was posed, it could not be undone. It gnawed at me like a hungry parasite. It cut into me with the cold, sick feeling of an executioner's blade.

And without moving a single muscle, I ran.

But no matter how I struggled to summon the way home, no matter how much I clicked my heels together and wished to steal away to the tower with this extraordinary man under my wing, nothing at all happened. It wasn't that *I* couldn't go home. I simply could not take Dare with me into a world that existed outside his present perceptual boundaries.

I could not take him *beyond* the world of matter and men until he was beyond the reach of Time and Death.

And since I had already acknowledged that he had ensorcelled me beyond all ability to reason, I could only lie there in the dark like a condemned man slated for the morning gallows.

Gee, what happened to The Quest for Emily? the beast asked, daring to taunt me at such a time.

"Emily," I muttered, and with a heavy sigh. Even the memory of this woman who had inadvertently been the mother of Umberlight seemed light-years distant.

My fitful thoughts and midnight murmurs must have awakened the blacksmith, for I felt him stir at my back. Sitting up, he gazed down at me in the pale moonglow.

"You all right, Thorn?"

I had bitten him to the blood and drank the living essence of him until he had fallen asleep in my arms, and he was asking *me* if I were all right.

I did not turn my head to look at him – for if I did, I was

afraid I would lose what little was left of my mind.

"I'm well and fine," I lied, but with enough conviction that he believed me. "Rest now. Sleep."

The command to sleep was one that I placed in his mind through the link that had been created when I drank from him.

He did not resist. He did not fight me.

Settling once again at my back, already halfway sleeping, he threw a possessive arm over my chest and pulled me to him until his lips were brushing my neck. The feel of him was so erotic I could barely maintain my grip on reality.

"I thought I'd imagined you," he mumbled, falling deeper into a restful slumber.

I kissed the hand that had been draped over my shoulder. "I'm here," I assured him. "You have my word."

His breathing was deep and slow as he drifted in the arms of alpha sleep. My promise seemed to comfort him.

"Mmmm," he murmured, warm breath of life on my neck. "I thought I heard you talking to Emily."

Everything went still. The moon had fled. The embers had died. The crickets simply stopped.

"You know Emily?" I finally managed to ask, though Dare was so close to sleep I wondered if he heard me at all.

For a long time, he didn't answer. When he did, it came with a hint of easy laughter. "She's my wife," was all he said, and then he was truly asleep.

I did not move. I could not have breathed if my preternatural body had required it.

Life in the World Above had just become a lot more complicated.

THE END

Book 2 in the series, "Tales of Umberlight" is currently in the works, and should be released in the fall of 2015.

ABOUT THE AUTHOR...

Alexis Fegan Black

Alexis Fegan Black is the award-winning author of many gay romance novels and short stories. Her writing in the genre began in the early 1980s and continues to this day. She has also written non-fiction books in the field of quantum metaphysics, and brings that sense of awe and mystery to *Prince of Umberlight*.

Alexis Fegan Black received the coveted Surak Award for 2 of her novels, and is a featured author in many prominent publications, both professional and underground. She was a pioneer in the early days of male/male or "slash" romance fiction, and is especially well-known for her award-winning trilogy, *Dreams of the Sleepers*.

Prince of Umberlight is her first fiction novel in many years, and represents a joyful return to her roots.

She is currently working on other books in the "Tales of Umberlight" series.

To read other works by Alexis, consider these...

www.fanzinesplus.com
http://archiveofourown.org/users/AlexisFeganBlack/works

Other fiction titles from Eye Scry Publications...

NO FORWARDING ADDRESS
Della Van Hise

When Terrans came to sail dark seas,
And see what stars might be...
Heaven moved with no forwarding
address,
And left this void to me.
(Children's song from Lazali)

_____

A literary science fiction novel told in the voice of an empath, *No Forwarding Address* explores the lures and the dangers of love, the tragedies and triumphs stirring in the human heart.

When Crystal and Raine first meet, it is 50 years after The Great War on Earth. They are hesitant to trust, afraid to love. But even if they are able to overcome these seemingly insurmountable obstacles, is even love enough?

When a man has the stars in his eyes, legend says he must serve them above all others.

_____

I knew then that it wasn't love and hate who were mirror twins. The final irony was that <u>grief</u> would always turn out to be the paradoxical antithesis and simultaneous manifestation of whatever it is that humans call love.

Crystal remained silent and walked a few steps away from Raine – further down the shoreline, until she stood under the wing of one fallen Phantom. She thought of the ship she had seen from the balcony of our home, and though it had long since disappeared over the dark and treacherous abyss of the ocean, its image lingered clearly in her thoughts. On that ship was a man, she thought. A terribly lonely man who made no great difference to the flow of time or the memory of the galaxy. A man who, like Raine, was compelled to keep moving and look only ahead and never behind. A man who could not afford the luxury of waving goodbye to friends on shore.

At last, she turned toward her beloved and watched him watching the darkness. He stood only a few feet away, yet the images in my mind said he might as well have been a million light years off in the void. He was lost to her in that instant out-of-time, just as lost and impossible to find as the light from that ship which had vanished over the horizon...

www.eyescrypublications.com
http://www.amazon.com/Forwarding-Address-Della-Van-Hise-ebook/dp/B00PEOSKJ0/

COYOTE
Della Van Hise

A Novel of Love, Honor and Personal Sacrifice...

When River Willows is accused of a murder she didn't commit, her life takes a turn toward the sanctuary of a world existing at right-angles to our own. Combining the mysticism of martial arts and the romantic conflict of a young woman torn between two powerful men, COYOTE takes the reader on an epic journey of dangerous secrets, military cover-ups, and the infinite heart of the peaceful warrior.

"So who's Coyote?" I asked, trying to ignore the effect he was having on me. "You?"

Steale laughed easily, though it did little to hide the torment behind that mask of indifference he wore so well.

"Coyote's a scavenger, Jack of all trades. The Native Americans call him the trickster - the one who brought chaos down on the world." He shrugged as if altogether unconcerned. "Original sin."

"Is that what you are?" I asked, keeping it light despite the growing knot my stomach. "Original sin?"

He kept his profile to me, eyes straight ahead as he drove. "Sure you want to know?"

I couldn't help wondering if I had cornered the coyote, or if the clever trickster had cornered me.

By the author of **KILLING TIME** – without a doubt the most controversial **STAR TREK** novel ever published!

From the author:
www.eyescrypublications.com

On Amazon
http://www.amazon.com/Coyote-Della-Van-Hise/dp/0976689782/

YEAR OF THE RAM
Della Van Hise

Year of the Ram was described by one reviewer as... "A spacefaring gay romance full of love, angst, and longing."

Only after Star Commander Morgan Diego becomes an exile as a result of a Galaxy Corps political blunder does he begin to realize how much he valued the companionship of his second in command - the mysterious Lucien, an Alfarian who is more elven than human, with peculiar powers & abilities which begin to unfold as he, too, realizes what he has lost.

Separated by circumstance from his former life, Morgan is thrust into a world where he must survive by his wits. When he meets a peculiar little old man calling himself Kim Le, Morgan finds himself in a situation where he is required to master The Art - not only a form of human & extraterrestrial martial arts, but a way of living and being that will alter his life forever.

At the temple, he is introduced to his new teacher, another Alfarian who begins to steal his heart - a heart which is already promised to Lucien. Torn and conflicted, Morgan struggles with the world he left behind and the world he now inhabits.

Beginning to believe he may never again return to his ship and to the friends and loved ones he left behind, he is all the more frustrated and heartbroken when a new Master arrives at the temple: a man to whom Morgan is immediately drawn both mentally and physically, a man who is strikingly familiar... yet utterly alien.

Year of the Ram is a fully-fleshed novel, approximately 97000 words, with a focus on the love story and romance angle. Set against a science fiction milieu, it explores the infinite possibilities of the human and alien heart. Sexual content is explicit, though is not the primary focus of the novel.

For those who like a romance that forces its characters to contemplate the ecstasies AND the agonies of love... you will enjoy *Year of the Ram* immensely.

FROM THE AUTHOR:
www.eyescrypublications.com
ON AMAZON:
http://www.amazon.com/Year-Ram-Della-Van-Hise/dp/0989693813/

LETTERS TO AN ANDROID
Wendy Rathbone

Cobalt is a created human, vat grown and born adult, with no human rights and indentured to serve others for the duration of his life. Liyan is a young man with wanderlust in his eyes, embarking on a career that takes him to the furthest regions of space. The two become unlikely friends and create a memorable long-distance correspondence. Through Liyan, Cobalt gets to explore the universe, living vicariously through his friend's wave transmissions. A strong bond develops between them that not even the stars can put asunder.

Now you know an android who writes poetry.

This is all your fault. Did you not read my last wave telling you extracurricular activities for my kind are discouraged? Of course this is harmless and strangely enjoyable and does not necessarily require me to leave the hotel. Pel would not care if I wrote lines of equations or nonsensical juxtaposed words. As long as the act does not bring my mental state into question.

However, in history, poetry is often written by the rebels.

So we can keep this to ourselves.

Let me know about your lieutenant's test.

And to give you peace of mind, I never believed you observed me as anything other than human.

Some people are and always will be hateful bigots. Most people are simply uncomfortable in speaking to "property." And anyway, friendship, like poetry, is also discouraged.

Your friend,
Cobalt

FROM THE AUTHOR:
www.eyescrypublications.com

ON AMAZON:
http://www.amazon.com/Letters-Android-Wendy-Rathbone/dp/0989693872/

PALE ZENITH
Wendy Rathbone
A Science Fiction Novel

On a far-flung "Earth" in a parallel universe, two factions are fighting a decades-long psychic war. Young talented psychics are being temporarily kidnapped from present day Earth, seemingly at random, to serve as part of one side's psychic army. They are put under the control of spychiatrists, mysterious machines with many limbs that have a programmed ability to travel time and space and universes to kidnap and control carefully selected humans. The humans never know they are being used; when their missions are completed they are brought back to their universe through time and placed back in their beds, their memories wiped.

The shadows wound the tall corridor in muted gold, varnished brown. It seemed as though they were in the bowels of a giant serpent coiled outside time, outside space.

When they left the palace, a familiar sun flourished in a clear, blue sky. But this wasn't their sun. Not Zack's sun. It was an alien star burning within a different galaxy in an all too distant universe. Zack looked up squinting, trying to see if he could peer beyond the sky, beyond the pale of midday and into his own timespace, but there was nothing. Only sunlight. Only the thin atmosphere of an Earth not his own.

His back knotted again. Leo's presence was a gelid space inside his chest, empty. Always before he'd felt a warmth there, a sort of pressure like someone's hand pressed gently to his heart. He'd taken Leo for granted knowing, the way a shadow falls when you block the sun, that he was there around him, inside him: blood, air, salt, brain, soul. They were genetic duplicates, twins, spiritual halves. Without him, Zack knew the first icy tugs of panic.

FROM THE AUTHOR
www.eyescrypublications.com
ON AMAZON
http://www.amazon.com/Pale-Zenith-Wendy-Rathbone/dp/0976689790/

Moltenrose
Stories Set in the *Pale Zenith* Universe
by *Wendy Rathbone*

In a post-holocaust world, a young woman and her robot partner leave their nomadic gang to take a long trek on foot to the city of Moltenrose to seek their fortune. **Green Forever** is a coming of age novella about love, death and making your own luck.

In the story **Moltenrose**, a deformed man whose nickname is 'Ugly' lives in the shadowed ruins of the barely-alive city and works in a sideshow at the tourist-trap carnival at the edge of town. His story involves several 'firsts' including a lesson about beauty.

Excerpt: *"You're late, boy," Rycoff mutters as I walk under the awning and into the tent. His belly hangs over an expensive gold belt, the vinyl trousers like a plastic sack he'd forced his flesh into. He wears a fashionable long-sleeved, bulky paper shirt. White. It sticks to his arms and back. There's already a little tear in it at the wrist. He goes through a dozen a day.*

"How can I be? There's no line yet."

"I pay you by the hour, Ugly. Try to remember." He shuffles by me, leaving a scent-trail of sweat and mint. The black skin of his face glistens. The white braid that flaps over his shoulder is as artificial as my half-wig. A stranger might take him for a clown, but he's as shrewd a business-person as Colere the trans-hop queen, who owns half the Free World. Rycoff's just had a little less luck.

I take Main Street to work every day. It needs mending, as does the entire city of Moltenrose. Ghost City, people call it. A fitting place for me since I'm just one more broken down part of it. And the carnival on the east side where tourism keeps what's left of it alive is as good a place as any to work.

On Amazon: http://www.amazon.com/Moltenrose-Stories-Pale-Zenith-Universe/dp/1942415001/

Our Site: http://www.eyescrypublications.com

The Foundling
by Wendy Rathbone

Diego is a powerful man with a tragic past. Out on the expansive ocean in his private yacht, he discovers a beautiful and mysterious man adrift on a raft, near death. The bond that forms between them in the aftermath of Alec's rescue is one of fierce passion, though lacking in trust. Can they make it work, or will Alec's amnesia bring forth secrets so disturbing as to tear them apart? A passionately erotic love story of desire and darkness, exquisite and explicit.

I can see his struggle between gratitude and uneasiness. He is buffeted by all things new and strange. He does not know where he is from, who he is or what happened to him. He does not know me. There has not been enough time to transition between strangers and friendship.

This isolation of his is something I can identify with, but it is also a feeling no one can help him with until or unless he gets his own life back. And his memory.

If that doesn't happen, then it will take time for him to build a new life. He is polite to me, even friendly, but even a night together during a storm with his arms wrapped tight around my waist doesn't calm the surge I see inside him, the emptiness, the loss, possibly even panic. That night may have reinforced some trust in me, but so far not enough for him to completely relax.

He seeks me out, though. That's something. He sits by me at dinner when he can have any seat of his choosing. I watch him closely when he does not realize it. At dinner the following night after we had only 'slept' together, and before we go to bed again in separate rooms, I notice everything about him, how he moves, the way the air warms when he is closer to me, the dry sheen of his lips as they part for more air when he is reacting to something, or speaking, or eating.

His hands still shake. Anyone else might not notice because he keeps them clasped into fists at his sides or, while sitting, pressed tight to his lap.

I spend another fretful night alone. I dream restlessly, wild, loud and colorful visions I cannot recall at all as soon as my eyes open. All I know is the dreams leave me unfulfilled, impatient.

www.eyescry.com/html/publications.htm

WENDY RATHBONE

None Can
Hold the Dark

None Can Hold the Dark
Wendy Rathbone

In the eagerly-awaited sequel to Wendy Rathbone's homoerotic romance ***"The Foundling,"*** Diego and Alec meet new challenges in private and from the outside world. Diego is being investigated by the local police for murder. Meanwhile, Alec's amnesia and the trauma of his kidnapping by white slavers continue to plague him. And the danger to Alec is not yet over.

Distracted by their new love, both men fail to see certain threats until it is almost too late.

"Why do you keep doing this illegal business?" Now Alec's gaze turned toward him, open as the day and lit with a sad frenzy, a challenge. "You could go anywhere, do anything, be anyone."

Diego had asked himself that question on rare occasions. In truth, he got used to what he was, what he did. Even a dangerous known was perhaps preferable to the unknown. "People depend on me."

Alec shook his head, but smiled a little as he said, "That's so weak." He leaned forward, over the arm of the chair, and put his shaking hand on the back of Diego's head. The kiss was cool, lingering, moist with salt. When Alec pulled back, he said almost matter of factly, "It's like there's sharks and there's goldfish and one can't decide to become the other."

Diego was still stunned by the kiss. But the words hit him hard. In them was the unfair conjecture of a locked fate. He believed in making his own fate...or luck. Did Alec think only one kind of man lived inside him and that was all there was to it? To life? It hurt. Badly.

Diego sat back on his heels, catching himself with his hands on the smooth floor. "So, Alec, which am I?"

Alec frowned.

Diego said, "I made choices in my life. I made them No one made them for me. If I need to be strong I'm strong. If I need to be vicious I can be that too. So what? I'm stuck there? In a pattern, a role...with no free will?"

Alec watched him inquisitively now.

"Because," Diego went on, "I'm solely responsible for my actions. Me. Could you say the same of the shark?"

They both waited, the silence covering them in muggy discomfort.

"You think you understand me?" Diego finally asked.

www.eyescrypublications.com

The Lostling: Alec's Story
Book Three in The Foundling Trilogy
by *Wendy Rathbone*

The Lostling takes place directly after *None Can Hold the Dark*, as Alec and Diego relocate to San Francisco. There, amid salty winter wind and fog, Alec's lost memories slowly return and he must relive some of his most painful and terrifying moments to regain his forgotten self. In agonizing dreams and flashes of memory, he finally remembers what happened to him... and why.

Excerpt: *Putting a hand on his arm or leg, I can always feel the tremor of Diego even through his clothes, an innate wildness, a life-power.*

I always believed, from the first day Diego found me unconscious and dying, floating in the middle of a sapphire Caribbean ocean, there was a core of me unhidden, unforgotten, that cried out silently to the air and everything around me communicating who I am, what I am.

I can't remember it myself. Not that core, not anything up to the day I awoke in Diego's bed, sick and panicked. In that moment, I remembered nothing more than my first name, and even that memory is suspect. But this core of me demands to take things into its own hands to be seen, to make sure it remains "I am."

I believe Diego saw it, the urgent desperation in me wanting to be witnessed, and he made a promise to that essence of me, to that heart of me, that he would see me through anything that came my way. Something in me reached up and latched onto him, a clasping energy, and Diego clasped back.

It caught and held him. He was moved. He was compelled. He was mesmerized.

www.eyescrypublications.com

http://www.amazon.com/Lostling-Alecs-Story-Foundling-Book-ebook/dp/B00RO8GSUW/

My House Is Full of Whispers
Wendy Rathbone

Ten erotica short stories by Wendy Rathbone - former winner of the prestigious WRITERS OF THE FUTURE contest!

Leda has not one beautiful man, but two. Kale enters a secret world in a wealthy man's basement. Noah is in love with a man who hates sex. Dina lives next door to a famous Hollywood director she secretly loves. Dorian has a sixteen year old female student coming onto him. Tara is haunted by an erotic ghost. Young Dimitri is kidnapped by lecherous men. And more.

Author's Preface

When I wrote these stories, I deliberately set out to gently break down certain barriers, and I've certainly broken taboos. Do I care? No. This is fantasy at its purest level. The stories are never meant to be political statements, nor do they make any attempt at political correctness, and there is little consideration for safe sex. While I definitely condone safe sex, my stories come from fictional realities in my head where safe sex is not much of a concern because, well, it's imaginary and it's fiction!

For me, these stories are meant as little poetic erotic ramblings merely to stir the flames of desire, nothing more. They are pure fantasy and therefore to be enjoyed as such. Every story is erotic in nature, meant to titillate, some more explicit than others. Some of the stories are light, some are darker. I invite the reader to a feast of diversity and delight.

One reader commented: *"...some of the most beautifully written erotica since Anais Nin!"*

FROM THE AUTHOR:
www.eyescrypublications.com
ON AMAZON:
http://www.amazon.com/House-Full-Whispers-Wendy-Rathbone-ebook/dp/B00IJK3G04/

UNEARTHLY
by Wendy Rathbone

A Collection of
Award-Winning Poetry

Intro by the Author: This book contains all my out of print chapbooks (mini-collections of an author's work usually published by smaller presses.)

The chapbooks published within include:
Moon Canoes, published by Dark Regions Press, 1994
(Im)mortal, published by Shadowfire Press, 1996
Scrying The River Styx, published by Anamnesis Press, 1999
Autumn Phantoms, published by Flesh and Blood Press, 2000
Dreams of Decadence Presents: Wendy Rathbone, published by DNA Publications 2002
Dancing in the Haunted Woodlands, published by Yellow Bat Review, 2003
Vampyria, published by Eye Scry Publications, 2005

She Sleeps With Vampires
She sleeps with vampires
courting velvet breaths
poem-dreams
chill-stopped hearts

Wrapped in her arms
like teddy bear thoughts
purple lips trembling
at her quiet throat
they love her more than
somber rain
more than autumn
more than ash-soft hearths of night.

FROM THE AUTHOR
www.eyescrypublications.com

ON AMAZON
http://www.amazon.com/Unearthly-Wendy-Rathbone-ebook/dp/B00B0MTIZK/

Non-fiction titles from Eye Scry Publications...

TEACHINGS OF THE IMMORTALS
by Mikal Nyght

So... You Want To Live Forever?
The teachings are presented as brief vignettes in no particular order of importance. This is not a book you read from start to finish in a single night. It is a grimoire of self-creation, intended to be contemplated slowly so as to be assimilated wholly. Pick it up and turn to a page at random. Where your eyes come to rest on the page is your lesson for the day. Go no further until you have assimilated the lesson totally.

The teachings are seduction as much as instruction. This is the way of The Dark Evolution.

The Ruby Slippers
The danger of the consensual continuum is that its natural gravity exists at the lowest common denominator of human experience, and because of this it will automatically make you forget those elusive truths you've fought to learn, and before you know it you're lost in petty dramas again, sinking into the mire of old familiar scripts.

The only way to overcome this is to be continually cavorting with worlds and events beyond human experience, journeying into the unknown so that it can become known, expanding knowledge and awareness to become more than you were, bringing back from the Dreaming those secrets which will teach you how to use the ruby slippers to transport yourself over the rainbow to the vampyre wizard's secret lair.

Perception
This is the nature of reality: to be precisely what perception dictates, as solid and whole as your interpretation of it, or as changeable and eternal as you permit it to be.

It wasn't knowledge god tried to keep from Man, you see. It was perception, for perception alone has the power to destroy god and obliterate comfortable consensual realities to create unending immortality.

Take the apple, my embryonic children. Nibble its red red flesh.

Open your vampyre eyes so you may finally begin to *See*.

www.immortalis-animus.com
www.eyescrypublications.com

http://www.amazon.com/Teachings-Immortals-Mikal-Nyght-ebook/dp/B00C2HY5WS/

Quantum Shaman:
Diary of a Nagual Woman
Della Van Hise

"Diary of a Nagual Woman brings a quantum understanding to what has traditionally been believed to be a mystical path alone. This book picks up where Carlos Castaneda left off to take us on a roller coaster ride of our own forgotten power..." - Michael Grove, Reviewer

When I asked how Orlando had known I would come to this remote location, and how he himself had gotten there – since there were no other cars in the tiny parking lot – he only smiled a little, stretched out his long legs, and slouched down on that cold metal bench to stare up at the stars.

"You're predictable," he said as if I should have already known. "I'm here because this is where you always come when you're mad at the world."

I attempted to engage him in a conversation of just exactly how he knew I was mad at the world, since I'd had no direct contact with him in quite some time, nothing to give him any hint of what was going on in my everyday life. But even as I began spelling all of that out to him, he brushed my words aside with an easy gesture.

"Do you want to talk or do you want to waste time looking for logical explanations for every magical thing that ever happens?" he asked. "That's what's wrong with the world, you know. Instead of embracing the mysteries and trying to determine how they might open a crack in an otherwise humdrum, pre-programmed existence, people waste their entire lives explaining it all away, attaching labels to it, filing and categorizing it until it loses any meaning."

He had a point. And I'd already been inundated with enough mysteries to know that some things simply had no explanation humans could understand. *'Magic is only science not yet understood'.* Words Orlando had written more than a year before rattled through my mind up there in the middle of the night, in the middle of nowhere, looking down on a distant world that seemed far more unreal to me at that moment than the world he had been trying to teach me to *see.*

He was there – whether physically or in some spirit-form is ultimately of no importance, for in the sorcerer's world there is no difference between body and spirit, and in any world, perception is reality.

www.quantumshaman.com
www.eyescrypublications.com

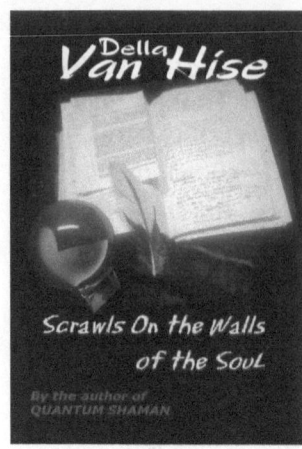

Scrawls on the Walls of the Soul
Della Van Hise

The long-awaited follow-up to
Quantum Shaman: Diary of a Nagual Woman.
Stands alone, or order together!

"If you've ever felt like a stranger in a strange land, this book is your road map to survival in the spiritual wilderness!" (Michael Grove)

~

It was May of 2000 when my mentor threw me out of the quantum cosmic classroom and said, "I've taught you everything I can. Now it's time to take that knowledge and slam it up against the walls of the real world. If it remains intact and survives the brutality to which it will be subjected, you will get a gold star next to your name and be allowed to proceed to the next level." No mention was made of what this next level might be, or if, indeed, it truly existed.

Go ahead – try to explain this all-consuming path to your friends and relatives. They will smile politely, squirm uncomfortably, and eventually they will stop returning your phone calls and look the other way when they see you coming. And who can blame them? They live in the real world with their office jobs and nuclear families and a host of mindless sitcoms waiting on the propaganda box at the end of their busy day. In direct contrast, it could be observed that anyone who has dedicated themselves to the pursuit of forbidden knowledge really doesn't live in that world at all. Not for lack of wanting, perhaps, but because the real world is quickly seen to be little more than a series of programs and illusions – not unlike The Matrix. And not surprisingly, the people who populate that world may begin to take on a peculiar zombie-like quality.

You find yourself alone in a world of jesters, jokers and jackasses. Now what?

FROM THE AUTHOR
www.quantumshaman.com

ON AMAZON
http://www.amazon.com/Scrawls-Walls-Soul-Della-Hise-ebook/dp/B008CUKH6C/

ENLIGHTEN YOURSELF!
The Art of Silent Knowing

Gnosis is the art of hearing the flame
Seeing the voice of the crow
Listening to the silent wisdom
of the sentient Infinite.

What is silent knowing? Simply put, it is learning to ask questions of that vast sentience which is the universe, the All, and simply the Self.

STOPPING THE INTERNAL DIALOGUE

Learning to stop the internal dialogue enables the warrior to get one step closer to permanent gnosis - the place of silent Knowing, where the entire library of Infinite Knowledge is at our disposal.

www.quantumshaman.com

CREATING THE DOUBLE

This is a power-packed exploration of what it means to create the double. Nitty-gritty how-to, exercises to motivate and validate. For warriors who are ready to turn and face themselves in the mirror of the Infinite, there is no better starting point, and there is no one on Earth more qualified to present this workshop than Della, whose interactions with her own double, have led her to fulfill her destiny as a nagual woman and teacher.

UNDOING THE PROGRAMS

This workshop gives you the tools for getting rid of belief systems that keep you from achieving your greatest success in this world, and may be preventing you from embracing your highest potential in the realm of Spirit.

"As long as a man truly believes he is powerless, he has no reason or motivation to seek the source of his own power." (Orlando)

Available on Amazon or from the author at
www.quantumshaman.com

Eye Scry Publications
A Visionary Publishing Company
www.eyescrypublications.com

www.ingramcontent.com/pod-product-compliance
Lightning Source LLC
Chambersburg PA
CBHW031345170626
46807CB00002B/828